The Bounty Hunter's Bride

I0674465

Janis Jakes

The Bounty Hunter's Bride
COPYRIGHT 2021 by Janis Jakes

Cover Art by *Nicola Martinez*
White Rose Publishing, a division of Pelican Ventures, LLC
www.pelicanbookgroup.com PO Box 1738 *Aztec, NM * 87410
White Rose Publishing Circle and Rosebud logo is a trademark of Pelican Ventures, LLC
Publishing History
First White Rose Edition, 2021
Electronic Edition ISBN 978-1-5223-0349-7
Paperback Edition ISBN 9781522303718
Published in the United States of America

Dedication

To my Lord, with gratitude for His never-ending kindness.

1

Sweat dotted Luke's brow, trickling down his temples in a ragged trail. If there'd been a hotter day in West Texas, he couldn't recall when. His swollen tongue clung to the roof of his mouth. Sticky granules of sand peppered his cheeks. Not a single tree in sight and only one watering hole for miles—the perfect place to capture a criminal.

Looked like a kid off in the distance but "wanted dead or alive" let Luke know to keep his guard up. Pistol in hand, he watched the lone figure—wondering what the kid would do next. Predicting the mind of an outlaw wasn't easy, especially one who was likely hotheaded.

The young man rested on his knees at the water's edge. He cupped his hands, bent to drink, and pulled off his hat. Copper hair tumbled down in a thick braid, stopping an inch or so above a slender waist.

Luke blinked.

The outlaw turned sideways, revealing curves.

Confusion overtook Luke's rational thoughts. He rubbed his eyes with his free hand. Maybe the desert heat was playing tricks on him. He looked again. Had the figure disappeared? He glanced toward the ground, rubbing his eyes once more.

The whirr of a bullet sliced through the air, knocking Luke's hat from his head. He leaped from his horse, taking cover behind a boulder. On instinct, his horse followed, partially hidden by the rock mounds surrounding his lookout position.

She fit the description—the trousers and shirt, the horse, everything. He tried to recall the face in the wanted poster. It had looked feminine, but he'd thought that was because of the age. Twenty-two years old and fresh-faced, but no mention of the word *woman*.

The name on the poster was Billie Batson, but he'd just assumed the variant spelling meant a man. He'd been duped. Bringing any woman in for justice wasn't something he intended to do. It was a silent code among those in his profession. Bounty hunters marked women as off-limits, though right this second, he wasn't sure why.

He squinted over the rock, holding his hand up to shield his eyes. His ears still rang from the bullet that almost took off his head. There was no sign of her. He squatted back down, unsure what to do next.

Get your wits together, man.

Luke inched upward once more. She was still gone. Vanished. As if she'd never existed.

A lump rose to his throat, momentarily cutting off his air. Had she been a mirage? He was hot. Parched. Tired. He'd heard of people seeing images that didn't exist in the desert. Maybe that's what happened.

"Drop your gun." A voice sounded behind him, feminine and ominously close.

He turned and his stomach clenched. A heavy groan slipped between his lips. How'd he let this happen? He could see the newspaper headline now: *Veteran Bounty Hunter Shot Dead by Woman.*

He could even picture the smirk on Laurence Magellan's face. The man already loved to write and publish crass stories about him—called him a barbarian, among other things. He'd probably devote the entire front page to bragging about how Luke Lancaster finally got what he deserved—and by a female, no less, which Laurence would point out made it doubly fitting.

Instead of dropping his gun, Luke's grip tightened. He held his weapon steady.

She dipped her chin downward. She was a pretty thing. If he was to be shot by a woman—

"Mister, you'd better drop that gun right now. I know you think you can outshoot me, but my trigger's cocked and ready. All I have to do is squeeze."

"True," he said, keeping his calm. This wasn't the first time he'd stood in front of someone holding a gun. "But if I'm dying anyway, I might as well die trying."

"No one will die," she said, her voice cool and smooth. "Least not if you do what I say."

"You're a criminal. Am I supposed to believe your word?"

"You got a choice?"

"Yeah. I can try to shoot you first as I already said."

She rolled her eyes. "And they say women like to argue." She took a step toward him, her blue eyes turning cold. "Drop the stupid gun. Right now."

"All right, all right." He dropped the gun, hoping he hadn't made the biggest mistake of his life.

"Who are you anyway?" she said. "Why are you following me? Did Caldwell send you?"

"Who?"

"Clovis Caldwell."

He dropped his hand at his side, wondering why she sounded so annoyed. If anything, she should feel kind of smug right now. Maybe even smile or giggle for outsmarting a professional hunter like himself. Instead, she was spitting bull nettles and angry at who knew what.

"I never heard of the man," he said. "I'm here with the Littleton And Clark Detective Agency out of El Paso, Texas."

"Bounty hunter?"

He didn't want to answer.

Her cheeks turned flaming red. "That lying, conniving, murdering, greedy—" She muttered a few more words he couldn't hear. "Now he has bounty hunters believing him. I've had it. Cooked goose. Done."

He held still. Would she take her anger out on him? Could he get his gun before she shot him? Why had he ever thought he wanted to bounty hunt?

She stopped in the middle of her tirade—her stare boring into his own. "Take off your holster."

"A bounty hunter never—"

"Now!"

He unbuckled his holster, holding still as the

leather fell in a loose heap at his feet. He felt naked and silly to boot. If he survived, he might change his mind about taking in a woman. This woman deserved to face the judge and jury.

"Just so you know, I never stole anything, and I never killed anyone." She waved her gun at the ground. "It was all Caldwell's doing."

How many times had he heard this familiar tune? Every outlaw he brought in was as innocent as a baby, to listen to them tell it. Still, he knew better than to act as if he didn't believe her. "Who is Caldwell?"

She snapped back to the present, her eyes narrowing. "Kick your holster over here. At my feet."

"If you're innocent, then why not come back? Clear your name." He was trying to buy time, but there was more than that. He wanted to know the answer. He'd never heard of a bounty on a woman dead or alive. She must've done something awful.

"You really don't know who Caldwell is, do you?" she asked.

A gunshot ripped through the air, crashing past his ear and into the rock with a thunderous boom. Shards of rock flew into the air, followed by faint white particles of dust.

Luke's gaze darted to his gun. He glanced at the woman. Fear riddled her face as she took off, stumbling over her own feet as she scrambled for cover.

Which way were the bullets coming from? He wasn't sure. One ricocheted off the rock near his head, zipping past his ear. Another zinged near his feet, slicing off into the distance. The idiots, whoever they were, couldn't hit a barn on a clear day and would probably kill him right along with the woman.

Her horse took off, disappearing into a trail of dust with reins flapping. Luke's horse bucked, stomped, and then bucked again.

He had to get out of here. If memory served him right, there was a cavern only a half a mile away, hidden in the rocks. The Comanche used it for a lookout while hunting buffalo. If he could get there, he'd be safe.

Luke grabbed his holster and buckled it back on, dropping his gun into place. He stuffed his hat on his head and then slid his foot into the stirrup as another bullet whizzed by, disappearing into the endless desert. From the sound of the discharge, the shooters were moving closer. He pulled up into the saddle, crouching down low. "OK, boy, let's get out of here—"

His horse bucked and pivoted, turning toward the rocky hillside as if knowing where to go. He loosened his hold on the reins just in time to hear a faint voice call out.

"Wait!"

Luke shifted. The woman sat between two rocks with knees bent, her right hand on her upper left arm. Blood seeped between her clenched fingers, darkening her shirt with a crimson stain.

"Don't leave me." Then, more faintly, "They'll kill me."

I can't take you. They'll kill us both.

She seemed to sense his hesitation. "I'm innocent."

He frowned. The last time he'd decided to be a Good Samaritan it had cost him more than he could bear. The wound in his heart had yet to heal—never would. The thought of helping a woman who'd threatened to shoot him moments ago was insane. Downright foolish.

"Hope you get the chance to prove it..." Luke said.

"Mister, please—"

His chest tightened, but something else happened, too—a sharp prick, like the thorns on a rose, snagged one of the few soft places left in his heart.

He could almost see his mother's face, kind and tender with faint wrinkles and golden ringlets hanging past porcelain features. Though she never spoke the words, he heard her as clearly as if she'd whispered right into his ear. *Is that the way I raised you? You're not a savage. You're a child of God.*

Luke yelled from the darkest recess of his soul—a guttural sound that did not come close to expressing his frustration. He jumped from his horse and rushed toward the woman. If he died, he'd die pleasing the one person on earth who'd ever shown him unconditional love. He used a boulder as a shield and glanced to where the woman sat only seconds before. There was no sign of her—only the smear of blood upon a large stone.

"Billie!" He yelled, hoping that was her name.

From only a few feet away, a pale hand slipped upward above the rocks and waved as if greeting a passing friend. She must've toppled over onto the dirt, which wasn't such a bad idea. It might have saved her life.

He ducked and swerved, feeling the heat of the bullets zipping past him. This had to be the most daring and most stupid thing he'd ever done. If God still cared about him, and he wouldn't blame Him if He didn't, now would be a pretty good time to let him know.

2

Something tight slid over Billie's upper arm, biting into her flesh and squeezing without letting up. She winced in pain but lacked the strength to protest. Strong hands moved under her body and lifted her limp form. Had she been captured? She tried to open her eyes, but the dizziness was too much. Her body was pulled against the warmth of human flesh. If this was death, she welcomed it. A masculine scent moved under her nose.

"Billie, stay with me." The voice sounded vaguely familiar. Then, more urgent. "I'm getting us out of here."

In the next instant, she was tossed like a sack of potatoes upon something hard...a shoulder? More bullets spewed forth—most whirring over her head. She wanted to hide, but there was nowhere to go. A bullet sliced into her hip—barely skimming the flesh but leaving a path of searing pain in its wake. She cried out in agony. More bullets zipped past her. How could she still be alive? Her insides rolled. Nausea swept upward but refused to spill forward. Breaths came in ragged, shallow gasps.

Her body lurched upward, lifted higher, and then

fell across a saddle. She could smell the horsy scent of leather. Her hip burned with unbearable pain. Darkness swept over her like a ferocious wave, pulling her into its depths. She didn't know if she was dying or passing out, but someone had come to help her. Whether she lived or died, she was not alone. She couldn't think of anything worse than dying alone.

~*~

Billie awoke to nightfall, made less ominous from the light of a full moon. The howl of a coyote sounded nearby. Her eyes felt gritty as she peered into the shadows of the Chihuahuan Desert below. She was high on the hillside amongst large rocks and sharply etched overhangs. Contorted shapes of boulders were strewn below the perch. It could not have been easy traversing the maze. Someone must've known the exact path.

Billie reached up, touching her swollen, blood-crusted bottom lip. She'd busted her mouth as she raced for the rocks, stumbling forward when the first bullet hit her in her shoulder. Her hip ached, but not too bad. It was odd that her mouth hurt more than the bullet wounds.

But how did she get in this cave?

Fear began to travel up her spine. Caldwell's men. They'd brought her here. She didn't want to imagine why. She sat up slowly, glancing back over her shoulder.

A lone man squatted nearby. He watched her like

a mountain lion about to pounce on a wounded rabbit. Angular planes etched into handsome features. Broad shoulders. Muscled legs. Hard expression.

The bounty hunter! Her holster and gun lay inches from his feet.

What now?

"Are you cold?" he asked in a flat tone.

She didn't answer.

"I can't start a fire, or they'll find us. If you need a blanket—"

Did he think she would stay here once he went to sleep?

"If you think you can make a run for it, Caldwell's men are still out there. Right where we left them. Waiting for you."

Was he trying to scare her?

"Don't believe me?" He pointed off into the distance. "See that flicker of light?"

Could the man read minds?

"That's their campfire," he said.

She glanced out into the darkness, barely able to detect the faint glow. Words moved up her dry throat. "How do you know it's Caldwell's men? How do you know it's not bounty hunters, like yourself?"

He shifted, a faint snicker parting his lips. The man was bigger than she remembered. Or maybe he only looked bigger because she felt so vulnerable.

"No bounty hunter is that bad of a shot."

"They hit me twice," she said, her voice growing stronger.

"They got lucky." He stood up, walked to his

horse. Dirt clods crunched beneath his feet. He pulled a canteen from the saddlebag and extended the container to her.

Billie took a long swallow, uncaring that water ran down her chin and onto her blood-stained shirt.

"Easy," he said. "You'll make yourself sick."

She took another sip and then handed it back to him. She wasn't quite ready to say thank you.

"Your wounds need cleaning." He drank after her then dropped the canteen into his saddlebag. "I'll take you to someone who can help."

Exhausted, Billie laid back. Her hip throbbed—the shock easing up and the pain escalating. Even if she did make a run for it, there was no way she'd get far. She glanced at her arm, eyeing the tourniquet still in place.

How had she got to this place in her life? Only a month ago, she'd lived a predictable life—teaching school, attending church, eating dinner with friends, and enjoying the occasional barn raising and quilting bee. Now, she was wearing a disguise, running for her life, and wondering if she'd survive the night.

Her mother had always said her meddling would get her in trouble one day. Well, that day had arrived. Her mother would not be pleased to know she was right. She would be horrified if she saw her now—dirty, smelly, and bloody.

A lump rose to her throat. She wished she could tell her family she was OK. She wished—Who was she fooling? She wasn't OK. She was alive, but that was about it. She tried to stay in the present and sort out a mess that made no sense, "How much are you getting for me?" She couldn't meet his eyes.

"What are you talking about?"

"The bounty. How much are you getting for me?"

A nighttime breeze swirled about the rocks and cacti. The sound of a hoot owl echoed throughout the canyon below. Then a chorus of coyotes yelped in the distance. Sounds that once frightened her now gave her comfort—reminding her she was still alive despite Caldwell's desperate plotting and planning.

"Didn't you hear what I said?" he asked.

She turned to face him.

"I'm taking you to someone who can help. Someone to look after your wounds."

"I don't need looking after." She sounded childish even to her own ears. She needed serious help.

Gazing at him through the misty glow of the moon's rays, she noted the slight smile on his face. High cheekbones. Dark eyes. Ink black hair. And lips just wide and full enough to soften an otherwise stony face. Even still, she didn't trust him. Bounty hunters weren't respectable lawmen. They shot people for greedy gain. As far as she could tell, that made him as bad as Clovis Caldwell. Maybe worse.

"I don't want any part of taking in a woman for bounty."

Billie frowned. Was he only saying words to trick her into lowering her guard? "Why not?"

His furrowed brow showed that he didn't want to answer.

She'd seen that same look on the faces of her

students when she asked them a hard question. And her students were probably worried. Unless Caldwell had convinced the entire town that she was a criminal. Then they'd be hurt that the teacher who professed to care about them had betrayed them all. The thought caused sudden heat to rush to her eyes. She reached up, wiping away the tear before it could fall.

"So, why don't you tell me what happened?" he asked, his voice rumbling deep and drawing. "How'd you end up here, running from the law?"

The law? Anger rose within her chest like flaming hot coals. No way she was telling this man anything.

After several seconds of silence, he walked back toward his horse, loosening the bedroll tied to the back of his saddle. "The desert gets cold at night." He tossed the scratchy wool blanket her way. "Might want to bundle up."

She caught the blanket and then opened her mouth to tell him thank you, but he turned his back before she could muster the words.

He walked to the other side of his horse and laid down.

Silence surrounded her, followed by the faint sound of the bounty hunter's slow breathing. How had he fallen to sleep so easy? Murderous men waited only yards away to kill her, and probably him, too. It made no sense that a soul could curl up in a blanket and rest as if tomorrow didn't matter. He had a very hard conscience or a very clear one.

Billie shifted slightly onto her good hip. Soon enough, she'd know if the bounty hunter was intending to get help. Would he even care if she were healed, wounded, or outright dead?

Silver stars dotted the blackness of the expansive Texas sky, glimmering beneath a full, white moon.

Had God forgotten her? She'd always believed He would never leave her nor forsake her. Yet she felt lost and forsaken. She'd never pictured this as the end of her days. She'd always believed she'd grow old as a teacher with a husband who farmed the land and a passel of grandchildren to warm her lap in her final days.

Now, she was wanted for the murder of an honorable man, accused of stealing miner's gold, and charged with taking another man's horse. Those who knew her would never believe the lies, but others who didn't, would doubt her innocence—especially when someone as powerful and convincing as Clovis Caldwell made his case with Sheriff McGregor standing beside him.

Trembling fingers reached up and touched her neck. She could almost feel the noose. Tears gathered in her eyes, and her throat cinched. With her hopes dashed and her faith in shreds, Billie pulled her elbow up to her face, muffling the cries that escaped between swollen lips.

~*~

Luke braced himself. Even with his knees bent, his spine stiffened. He'd fallen asleep quick enough, but in his business, he never slept hard.

Whimpers had awakened him, followed by barely audible sobs then whispered prayers that gave way to more sobs. Billie could cry a river if she wanted. He wasn't feeling sorry for her. The woman had shot at him, and even made him drop his holster. Besides, he'd made that mistake before with another female, and it haunted his heart to this day. Never again. There was only one reason Billie wasn't headed to jail right now—his mother.

Luke lay still, listening for what seemed like an eternity as faint cries continued to chafe his soul. Like layers of hardened dirt rubbed from a gold nugget, his resolve began to sift away. An unexpected feeling emerged...*compassion*. The feeling was something long buried, something he never expected to have again. And, for reasons he couldn't grasp, with compassion came anger. Anger at the world, anger at himself, and yes, anger at Billie. It didn't matter whether she deserved it or not, it was there.

3

Billie opened her eyes, and then closed them against the bright morning sun. But she couldn't lay around forever, so she opened her eyes again and rose up on her elbows.

The bounty hunter's sleeping spot was empty except for a pair of worn boots.

She sat straight up despite the pounding in her skull. Her hand rested on her stomach—a queasy sensation filling her senses. She held still until the nausea subsided and inspected her surroundings. The air felt cool. After the searing heat of the last few weeks, she welcomed the relief—the crisp breeze, the scent of pine, and even the faint aroma of fire off in the distance.

Wherever the bounty hunter had gone, he left his horse behind to munch on grass. The only other things he'd left behind was his canteen and a packet, probably pemmican—both sitting near where she slept. Was this his way of being kind, or was something more sinister going on?

A vision of a young doe being lured into a trap laced with corn came to mind. Billie hesitated, but her stomach overrode her worry. She unwrapped the paper, and looked at the pemmican, giving it a good sniff before taking a large bite. She winced as her swollen lip reminded her to go easy. The dried bison brought her taste buds back to life with its savory tang. She would endure the pain for something in her belly.

Her hip felt better, and her arm, too. She glanced down, thankful to see the tourniquet gone. Blood crusted over the wound where the bullet had entered her arm. She examined it, afraid to touch it for fear it would start bleeding again. While still painful, it was bearable. With hands that trembled from weakness, she lifted the canteen, taking a drink. Her stomach tightened, but she didn't intend to let nausea win.

The muted sound of footsteps drew her attention. She twisted and looked out over the desert, her heart racing.

The bounty hunter appeared—a small, dead rabbit in his hands.

"How'd you—?" She could only stare in amazement. He was barefooted. She'd never known a person who caught a rabbit with their hands, let alone barefoot.

"We've got a good day's ride ahead of us. We both need something to eat. Especially you."

Billie's worry pushed through her gratitude. "Did you see any sign of Caldwell's men?"

He pulled his knife from his belt and began skinning the rabbit. Billie would've turned her head, but something about his skilled movements kept her attention on his hands.

"They're gone. Best I can tell, they're headed back

to town."

Hope soared. "You think they've given up?"

Luke gave her an annoyed glare. "Do you?"

No. Of course not. "Probably getting more supplies and more men." Hope plummeted.

"That's what I figure." He resumed his skinning, making quick work of it. "Let's eat so we can get out of here." He wove a sharpened stick through the meat and placed it over the flames, positioning both ends of the stick on the rocks to keep it off the direct fire. "We don't have much time."

He sounded as if he was helping her, but bounty hunters only cared about one thing: money.

The small amount of meat cooked in mere minutes. Though it smelled delicious, her stomach would only allow her to enjoy a small portion. The bounty hunter didn't seem to mind, eating his share and working on what remained of hers.

"I found something else while I was out looking for food," he said.

It seemed strange that they were having a civil conversation—like two acquaintances who happened to run across each other in town on a Sunday stroll. Less than twenty-four hours earlier, they'd faced each other with guns drawn.

"Your horse."

"My horse?" A smile burst across her lips.

"Yeah. She's grazing outside the cave."

Billie's guilty conscience pricked. "She's not exactly my horse. I...borrowed her from the livery stable."

He gnawed on the last piece of meat, stopping long enough to stare at her. "Borrowed?"

"Yes. Borrowed. I fully intend to take her back—as soon as I can."

He tossed the bone over his shoulder, wiping his hands down his pant legs. "Are you ready to tell me what happened? Why you're wanted?"

She glanced past him, deep into the cavern's darkness. She couldn't tell this stranger. For all she knew, he was showing her kindness to weaken her resolve and make her believe he cared. "I'm innocent. That's all I've got to say." Her tone was hard, but she didn't care.

He stood up, kicking dirt onto what remained of the smoldering fire. He was angry—the clenched jaw, the hard glare, the tight shoulder muscles—but he kept his voice monotone. "Think you can walk?"

"I can try."

She tried to stand but froze halfway up. Her head swam and the hip throbbed. Luke moved to stand behind her. He slid his hands under her arms and offered support as she attempted to straighten her legs. Instead, her knees buckled, and a groan parted her lips. She hated looking so weak—especially to this man.

Luke braced Billie with his body, his voice an urgent whisper. "Hold still. Don't try to walk. Just stand."

She crumpled, tears threatening to spill over. "I can't. I feel...faint."

"No." He put his hands around her waist, holding her up. His words came in a hot whisper only inches from her ear. "You've got to ride, Billie. Those men are coming back, and they'll kill you."

His words brought an abrupt stiffness to her spine—an icy splash of reality. She twisted around, facing him with only inches separating them. Her hands rested upon his shoulders for support. She'd never been this close to any other man, and her senses exploded. Every part of her wanted to move away from him but if she dared take a step—

Lord, help me.

His eyes blazed in seething anger that made no sense to her. It wasn't her wish to be in such a predicament. Could the man not show an ounce of mercy? "What's your name?" she asked in her demanding, schoolmarm tone.

Confusion caused his countenance to grow even darker. "What?"

"I can't call you bounty hunter. What's your name?"

"Luke Lancaster." He lifted her into his arms, carried her outside the cavern, and placed her on a nearby boulder. "Stay here."

He went into the cavern, came out with a rope, and then disappeared into the cacti-infested brush. A few seconds later, he reappeared with her horse.

Billie stood, wobbled, and then held steady.

Luke approached with a wary eye. His sturdy hands lifted and sat her in the horse's saddle.

"Ow!"

One dark brow jumped. "What?"

"Nothing. I'm fine. My hip—"

"Sorry." He sounded as though he meant it. "I'll be more careful next time." He placed the rope around her waist, looped it across the horn, and secured her in the saddle seat. "If you faint, you won't fall."

He disappeared inside the cave and returned on his horse. He secured the loose end of the rope to his saddle horn and glanced back at her with something close to kindness.

It was a new expression on his face, and one she welcomed.

"Ready?"

The pain in her hip had eased. She nodded, glad to move on. She was tired of feeling like a sitting duck. "I'm ready."

~*~

As dusk neared, Luke slowed the pace. Boulders had disappeared from the landscape, replaced with gangly mesquite, pine, and an occasional oak. "We're almost there."

Billie wasn't sure where *there* was but looked forward to getting out of the saddle. Her life was on the line, but she needed a rest. Tomorrow she'd be sore.

"You're not used to riding, are you?"

"I'm a schoolteacher. There's not much need to ride for hours on a horse. I usually spend my days in the classroom."

"Teacher? That's hard to believe."

He could believe what he wished. Her scruffy

appearance and pulling a gun on him hadn't helped win his trust. But who cared what he thought? The man was a bounty hunter. He had no right to judge her at all.

She let her horse pull away. She would rather follow from behind then ride next to him and carry on an annoying conversation.

The horizon had transformed from a deep blue to a dense gray with streaks of melon gold and pink marking the landscape. Mesquite limbs, dark and bare, etched a web across the dusky sky. The horses wove in and about the branches, ducking and bobbing to keep from getting snagged.

Luke had removed the rope that kept them connected, seeming confident she would not fall. She sat up straight for most of the ride, only asking him to stop twice so she could reposition her weight. He'd offered pemmican and water at one of their stops, which she gladly accepted. Despite his unexpected kindness, she didn't know what to think of him.

He drew his horse to a stop, waving her up next to him.

She gave the horse a slight nudge, looking out over the valley below.

A single cabin sat in the middle of a field encircled by trees. A couple of horses trotted about a fenced area, circling a cow and half-full pond. A small shed sat near the cabin, probably a root cellar. An illuminating kerosene lamp shone from the cabin's window, beckoning them forward. The quaintness of the imagery soothed her soul.

"We're here."

"It's lovely," she said, looking about the wide valley. "Where exactly is here?"

"You'll see." He flicked the reins and headed down the sloping trail that led to the cabin.

Please, Lord, don't let this be a trap. Let this be a place of refuge.

4

Luke whistled as they rode closer toward the cabin. The shrill, unexpected sound caused Billie to jump and her grip on the reins to tighten. Her horse came up off his front legs, landing hard.

"For goodness' sake," she spat between gritted teeth, her hand covering her hip wound. "Couldn't you have warned me?"

"Warned you about what?" He whistled again.

"That," she snapped.

Her horse lifted its head back with a jerk and a snort.

"Sorry, but if I don't give the signal, she might blow our heads off." He glanced over his shoulder. "I've dodged enough bullets over the last couple of days to last me a lifetime." He turned his head back to the cabin. "Except she wouldn't miss."

"She who?"

He didn't answer, easing his horse closer to the cabin.

A woman holding a baby stepped outside, contentment written across her smiling porcelain features. Golden hair framed her delicate face, the tresses lifted upward in a bun, and escaping in flighty wisps. Brown eyes gazed at her with open curiosity. The woman was attractive and several years younger than Luke. Perhaps his wife?

Excitement filled her gaze. "What a welcomed surprise."

"Abigail," he began, nodding toward Billie. "I've brought you a patient."

"Really?" She tilted her head. "She doesn't look as if she needs doctoring."

"A bullet hit her in the arm, and another grazed her hip." His tone lowered in concern. "The one that passed through her arm is starting to ooze."

"Clear or green?"

"Clear," he said. "For now."

"Good. Maybe we caught it in time so she can keep her arm."

"I might lose my arm?" Billie stared at the woman, aghast.

"It's always possible," Abigail said. "But with my doctoring skills, it's not probable." She offered a reassuring smile that did little to give Billie comfort. "We'll go inside. Luke can take care of the horses."

Billie eased out of the saddle. She slid off the horse and landed on the ground. Her stamina felt fine, though her stomach churned a bit after hearing her arm was in danger. But she would take whatever doctoring might come her way. Not that life without an arm was intolerable, but she would prefer to keep hers attached.

"How's Henry, Jr., doing?" he asked, reaching out for the reins. "Looks as if he's sleeping better."

"Yes, much better," Abigail said. "But I'm still worried about him. Can't get his fever to break for more than a few hours at a time, and he's not eating all that much."

Henry, Jr.? That didn't sound like Luke's child.

Abigail moved down from the steps. She placed her free arm gently around Billie's shoulders. Despite the other woman's frailty, her fingers felt strong—like someone used to hard work. Kindness permeated her presence. "Can you walk? You look a little pale."

"She lost a lot of blood," Luke said.

Abigail dropped her arm. "Why don't you carry her inside for me?"

"No," Billie stated, embarrassed.

Abigail's gaze latched onto her.

"I can walk fine."

"If you're sure..." Abigail glanced toward Luke. "Come on in after you get the horses settled, and I'll heat some stew. There's a little left, along with a bite or two of bread." Her eyes shone as they turned toward Billie. "Can't tell you how good it is to have you here. I get lonely this time of year."

This isn't exactly a social visit.

Luke's gaze shifted toward Billie. "She'll talk your ear off if you let her."

Billie wondered what the woman meant but didn't ask. She hoped to get stitched up and then be on her way.

"Oh, you hush," Abigail said. "Just cause you like being alone twenty-four hours a day doesn't mean everyone does." Abigail walked up the steps and inside behind Billie.

The small cabin was cozy with dim light from the kerosene lamp sitting in the center of a kitchen table. A cradle rested near the hearth. The woman laid the babe down with a gentle sweep.

Off to the side of the main room was a single bedroom. Billie looked about, ready to stretch out and rest.

"I have a mattress out in the barn where my last patient slept." Abigail patted the baby on the back for several seconds until he nestled in and grew still. "I'll get Luke to bring it in for me."

"That's too much trouble. I can sleep in the barn."

"Don't be silly," Abigail answered. "My last patient was a man. Without Henry here, he had to sleep there." She pulled out one of the dining table chairs and held Billie's elbow as she lowered to the seat. "My husband worries about my safety, though there's never been a reason. You're a woman, so I'm trusting I'll be fine with you. Besides, if you sleep in the barn, you'll be sleeping with my brother."

Billie heard the subtle threat, but the woman was making a point while teasing her in the process. "Luke isn't your husband?"

Abigail grinned, stifling a giggle. "Not even close."

"I see."

"Would you like a cup of water?" Abigail had already started pouring from the pitcher. "I just drew some for myself and the baby."

"Yes, thank you."

"I look like my mother, and Luke looks like our

father." She handed Billie the cup. "We never really knew our father, not much anyway. I can remember seeing him once or twice when I was much younger, but he never stayed long. We lived with our mother and grandparents."

"I'm sorry to hear that."

"I'm not complaining. It was a good life."

Billie nodded and let Abigail speak. She'd had a couple of students who liked to talk. She wished she could return to those days where her biggest problem was hushing talkative children.

"My grandfather had a horrible stutter," Abigail continued. "He was used to the cruelty of people, so he and Luke got along well. Our grandfather taught Luke to ignore the hateful comments of others, and my mother taught him to forgive them."

Billie took a sip of water. "What sort of comments, or is that too nosey?"

Abigail's hands lifted to her hips. "You don't know?"

"Know what?"

"Luke is Comanche, well, half Comanche. Our father was full-blooded."

"No, I didn't—" She blinked, trying to regroup.

How could she have not seen that? The skin tone, the black hair, the dark eyes, and the high cheekbones. The way he hunted barefoot. The secret cavern he hid them in. So many things made sense now, even things she hadn't questioned.

"Don't worry. You'll never find a more honorable man. Hard-headed, self-composed, and logical to a fault, but he'll always do the right thing. Can't help himself."

Billie replayed the memory of him almost leaving her to Caldwell's posse. A twang of guilt stirred her insides. She'd made him drop his guns. Most men would have left her behind to fend for herself. They'd assume she deserved death. If not for Luke, she'd be dead right now. He'd helped her. Reluctantly, but he'd still helped.

The baby whimpered. Abigail moved to his side — her eyes overflowing with love. Henry, Jr., lay with legs curled underneath him and one fist curled near his tiny mouth. He grew quiet, as if sensing his momma's presence.

"He's so small," Billie said. "How old is he?"

"Almost four weeks. He came early." She pulled the blanket up around the baby's chin, folding it over and tucking it in to keep him snug and secure. "So, what's the story between you and my brother? How did you end up together?"

Heat burned her cheeks. "There isn't a story between us, and we're not exactly together. There were men trying to kill me. Your brother brought me here. We've barely shared twenty words between us."

The sound of Luke's footsteps shuffled onto the front porch then moved inside, stopping the conversation from going any farther.

"Would you mind bringing in that straw mattress that's in the barn?" Abigail gave Luke an apologetic smile. "I need a place for my patient to rest. And, Luke, I hope you don't mind sleeping in the loft tonight…"

"Beats a cave," he said, heading back out the door.

"Would you like some stew?" Abigail asked.

Billie's mouth watered. It had been weeks since she'd had a home-cooked meal. "That would be wonderful."

"You have an appetite. That's a good sign."

Billie sat at the dining table opposite Luke, neither saying much as they ate every last drop of venison stew. They both took the small portion of their bread and raked the juice from the inside of the bowl, behaving like two people stranded at sea and finally enjoying a meal.

"I can't tell you how good that tasted." Billie smiled at their hostess.

"Yes," Luke said, standing up. "Thank you. And now, I'm calling it a night."

"We'd better all get some rest," Abigail said. "But first, I've got some doctoring to do." She looked at Luke and pointed toward the rocking chair. "Have a seat while I check out your friend."

"My name is Billie Jo Batson," Billie spoke in a soft tone.

"Billie Jo. That's a mighty fine name." Abigail turned toward the kitchen counter. She ground something in a small bowl. "Root bark," she murmured as she added white gel from an agave plant that sat near the window and stirred until it formed a thick goo. She placed the concoction on the table and rolled Billie's shirt sleeve up to reveal the wound. "What on earth did you do to get yourself shot up?"

"I'd rather not say."

"That's your business, I guess." She frowned, clicked her tongue, and turned to her brother. "Luke, bring a rag dipped in warm water. It's heating over the fire. I need to get our girl cleaned up."

"You told me to sit."

"Don't start misbehaving."

"Typical woman. Can't make up her mind...sit, get, stand, lay."

"Just cause you're older doesn't mean you're meaner," Abigail threatened, though laughter shone in her barely contained grin.

They were like so many siblings she'd taught. One minute they were loving and grateful to see one another and in the next, baiting and bickering—almost asking for a fight.

Luke returned a few seconds later with a warm cloth.

With a feather-like touch, Abigail wiped across the wound, and then swiped back and forth until every ounce of dried blood was washed away. She set the rag aside, examining the bullet entry point. Probing fingers pressed a little too hard.

Billie winced.

"Sorry," Abigail said. "I'm checking for infection. It looks as though the wound is inflamed, but not horribly so. I think we can get rid of any problems with several days of salve and some soap."

"Several days?" Billie exclaimed. "I'd hoped to be gone this time tomorrow."

"Not if you plan to keep your arm." Abigail paused, gazing into Billie's disappointed expression.

"Rest tonight. In the morning, you can take a bath."

"Do I smell bad?" Billie asked, already knowing the answer.

"Like a dead raccoon," Abigail said.

Billie laughed, surprised by the unexpected honesty.

Luke glanced her direction, his eyes smiling though his expression stayed blank.

"Now, I need to check out your hip." Abigail looked at Luke. "We'll need some privacy."

"Gladly. I'm going to bed." He stomped out of the cabin.

"What's his problem?" Abigail asked. "He's not usually so grumpy."

"He doesn't like me," Billie said.

"He doesn't like many people," she responded. "With good reason."

Billie didn't want to know more. She wanted to get fixed so she could leave—ride far away from Texas, Caldwell, and Luke. She had an aunt in Arkansas who would open her doors if she could get there in one piece.

"You can sleep in those clothes tonight," Abigail said. "Tomorrow, I'll burn them and get you something clean to wear."

"Thank you. But are you sure we shouldn't wash them? I might need them again."

"They're too blood-stained. They'd be a dead giveaway that you were shot up. Now turn on your side," Abigail said. "Slide your trousers down past your hip. I need to see where the bullet got you."

Billie did what she asked, surprised at her lack of embarrassment.

Abigail drew a magnifying glass from off a nearby table, examining the wound further. "Not bad at all," Abigail said. "Only a nick. I can fix that one in no time." She proceeded to put salve on the wound, covered it with a clean cloth, and tugged Billie's trousers over it to hold the bandage in place.

A yawn escaped Billie's lips. "Sorry…"

"No apologies needed. Get some rest. Food in your belly and a good night's sleep will do greater good for your body than any doctoring I might do." Abigail drew a blanket from the hearth ledge, draping it on Billie's legs. "Remember to say your prayers."

Billie had said plenty of prayers over the last few weeks, hoping and expecting answers that had yet to come.

As Abigail turned away to leave her side, Billie reached out and touched her hand—stopping her. "Thank you. For everything."

Abigail smiled with such love that tears warmed Billie's eyes. "Thank the good Lord. He's the One Who brought you here."

The simple words stayed with Billie all night and though sleep came swiftly, anytime she awoke to roll over and get more comfortable, she recalled what Abigail had said. Maybe her prayers were being answered after all—just not the way she expected.

5

"If he were a chicken, I'd wring his neck!"

Billie sat up, awakened by Abigail's outburst, and pushed wayward strands of hair off her face. "What's going on?"

"Luke rode out without so much as a good-bye. My brother is the most inconsiderate, stubborn, hard-hearted—" She stopped in the middle of her tirade, picking up baby Henry and immediately changing her tone to one of tenderness. "You'll not be like him when you grow up will you, my little man?"

A strange discomfort tugged upon Billie's heart. "Luke didn't say good-bye?"

"He did not." The angry Abigail returned. She placed Henry across her shoulder and patted his bottom with a tender thump. "I went to gather some eggs and check on him. He left."

The bounty hunter was out of her life and all worries of him turning her in for money were gone. But the thought unnerved Billie. She felt safe with Luke around. Anxiety lodged in her chest. What had she hoped would happen? That Luke would travel with her to Arkansas to make sure she got there alive? How ridiculous was that? He didn't owe her anything—

certainly not safe passage to another state. Still, she never expected abandonment.

His sister fed him, gave him a place to sleep, and welcomed him into her home with a loving heart. He'd acted as if none of that touched him.

"Maybe he didn't want to wake you." Billie had no idea why she was making excuses for the man. He deserved a good tongue lashing.

"It never stopped him before."

The baby began to wiggle and fuss. Abigail moved to the rocking chair, offering his hungry lips a full breast, and then covering herself with a small blanket. As Henry nursed, she looked toward Billie with a radiant smile. "I think having you here is good for Henry, Jr. He hasn't had a fever all night long, and he's hungry again."

That had nothing to do with Billie, but she liked to hear it. "Do you want me to scramble the eggs you brought in?"

"That depends. How's your arm doing this morning?"

"Whatever you put on it must've helped. It's not near as tender."

"Good, then scrambled eggs sounds mighty fine. There are potatoes in the root cellar if you want to bring them in."

She rose to leave.

"By the way, who is Malcolm?"

Billie's stomach dropped and her body turned cold. How did Abigail know about Malcolm? Her insides trembled, though she refused to show her outward emotions. "Why do you ask?"

"You called his name several times during your sleep. I thought maybe a beau—"

"A dear friend," she said, and prayed her heart wouldn't burst. "Need anything else from the root cellar, or will potatoes do?"

"Potatoes will do for now."

~*~

Billie prepared the meal with eagerness, glad to occupy her mind and feel useful. Today was Sunday—the day she typically helped her mother in the kitchen. She wondered how her parents were holding up.

Though their faith was strong, they'd endured one heartache after another over the past year. They'd suffered the loss of a daughter and a grandson in childbirth, a son who moved off to San Francisco chasing gold, another son married to a harsh woman who rejected God, and now—a daughter wanted dead or alive. Billie spooned the eggs and buttered potatoes onto plates as her mind wandered.

"Did you hear what I said?" Abigail asked.

"I'm sorry. My mind was adrift."

"Henry is almost asleep. I'll make us a cup of coffee in a minute or two."

"When is Henry, Sr., coming back?" Billie asked, setting the plates on the table.

"In a couple of weeks." Abigail put the baby in his crib and then placed the coffeepot on the stovetop. "Henry is a quiet and gentle man. I think you'll like him. He makes axes and knives and takes them about the countryside every few months selling his wares. I miss him something awful, but I knew what he did for a living when I married him. He's rather famous around these parts for his work. You'll be quite impressed."

Billie glanced down at her plate. She refused to keep secrets from Abigail. "I won't be here in a couple of weeks to meet him. I've got somewhere to go."

A furrow tugged on Abigail's forehead. "You have to get well before you go anywhere. If you open that wound again, who'll be there to put you back together?"

"I'll give it another few days." She kept her voice firm, wanting Abigail to know that the plan was not open to debate. "I've got family in Arkansas."

"That's not wise, Billie. A woman traveling by herself. Too many things could go wrong."

Billie kept her expression blank. *How much more wrong could things go?*

"I'll pray you reconsider," Abigail added.

Despite the shiver than ran up her spine, Billie gave her a faint smile. The woman's desire for her to stay came from a place of kindness, concern, and loneliness. Abigail had no idea what might happen if Caldwell's men found out she was here. They would kill them both, and the baby, too.

She already felt responsible for one person's death. She did not want to be the cause of more lost lives.

~*~

Luke rode hard, finally reaching El Paso in the early morning hours. More than once, he paused long enough to check his surroundings—sensing someone was following him but seeing no one. If Apache were on Luke's trail, he would be as good as dead. If Comanche, it would depend on their mood at the time. He knew it wasn't Caldwell's men; they lacked the stealth of the natives or the finesse of the bounty hunters. He would have seen them by now.

He shifted in his saddle and checked over his shoulder once more. The sunrise across the dark, rugged mountains stirred memories of times with his father and his Comanche brothers. He had ridden with them in peace as a young boy. Sometimes he wished he could get that back.

The whistle of a train drew his mind to the present and the task before him. Since the railroad arrived a few years earlier, a transformation had taken place in El Paso. Buildings rose out of the ground almost overnight, and more and more people arrived every day. What was once a lawless town riddled with vagrants and mischief-makers had become a respectable community where commerce thrived and families grew roots.

El Paso was also the home of the newest Littleton and Clark Detective Agency office and a regular stopping point for Luke to collect his orders and his pay.

The building sat in the middle of town—nondescript and dull against the backdrop of tantalizing smells, beautiful senoritas, colorful bonnets, light-hearted music, and wealthy entrepreneurs. Inside the building was equally plain—wood floors, bare windows, and minimal furnishings. Everything about the place contrasted with the vibrancy of town, letting any visitor or passerby know the serious view they took when it came to business matters.

Even with the windows raised, the hot Texas sun crushed the building with its relentless heat. Wide rings of sweat covered the underarms of the few men who worked inside.

A man greeted him with an outstretched hand. Theo Granger was in his early forties with wavy blond hair and a handlebar mustache tinged with silver. By all accounts, he was an intelligent man with a quick wit and a way with the ladies—all of which made Luke unsure if he should trust him or not. He'd only been the office director for a couple of months but let everyone know this was only a short stop to bigger and better things. That was another reason not to give him complete allegiance, in Luke's mind.

"Luke Lancaster." Theo greeted him with a somber expression. "Glad to see you again. Hope you've got good news for me."

"That depends," he said. "I want to know about the outlaw you have me chasing."

Theo dotted the sweat from his brow with a handkerchief. "I've told you all I know. If you've learned something new—"

Several men roamed about, all moving with a purpose. One scurried to his office. Another walked past with a bob of his head and papers in his hand. It was business as usual, but Luke intended to interrupt their day.

"Then tell me again," Luke said.

"All right." The man eyed him with suspicion. "Want to step into my office?"

Luke followed, taking a seat on the other side of a table that Theo used for a desk.

"I had the report out this morning," Theo began, scratching his head. "Re-reading the documents and checking with the sheriff to see if anyone had found our outlaw. This is a major case for Littleton and Clark, you know." He peered at Luke with a stern set to his jaw. "My reputation is at stake."

A tightness pressed Luke's lips together. "Read me the description of the criminal. Please."

Theo blinked. "Why?"

His jaw clenched as frustration rose. "You hired me to do a job, didn't you?" When Theo only stared, Luke added, "I want to hear the description again."

He shrugged. "Very well. Not sure where you're going with this, but—" He drew the file from the corner of his desk, opened it and read with slow, meticulous care. "Billie Batson. Slight of build. Strawberry-blond hair. Blue eyes. Wanted dead or alive for murder of a bank employee and theft of gold. Armed and dangerous." He handed the report to Luke. "Want to take a look yourself?"

Luke scanned the page. "That's all you've got?"

Theo shuffled through several papers before reading once again. "Says here that he killed a clerk he befriended at a local bank, making off with a chest containing ten thousand dollars of gold bullion belonging to miners."

Luke leaned back. "I don't believe it."

Theo blinked, the papers slipping from his fingers onto the desk. "You don't believe what?"

"Any of it. Who gave the report?"

"The report came from the insurance company that hired us to recover the money, but—" Theo looked down at the paper, one brow dipping downward as the other rose. "It's signed by a Sheriff August McGregor."

"No mention of a man named Clovis Caldwell?"

Theo scanned the paper again. "No." Impatience clipped his words. "Make your point, Lancaster. I don't have all day to play guessing games. What's going on, and what is it you don't believe?"

Luke leaned in, laying his forearm across the man's desk. "Billie Jo Batson is a woman. Your information is purposely misleading."

Surprise slapped across Theo's features like a splash of cold water. Complete silence enveloped the gulf between them for several seconds before he finally spoke. "A woman?"

"Ask yourself a question," Luke said. "How could one woman make off with a chest that a full-grown, muscled man would break a sweat trying to lift?"

With a flip of his wrist, Theo closed the file. "Woman or man, it doesn't matter. Bring the criminal in alive if you want. He or she will get their day in court." Theo leaned back, propping his foot up on his knee. "But first, I want to know exactly how you found out our outlaw was a woman?"

Luke didn't intend to give any ground. At this point, he wasn't sure who he could trust—and that included Theo. "I have informants."

"Informants lie, make mistakes, send you on wild chases."

"Not this one. It's true. Truer than that file you've got on your desk."

Theo's hard stare met Luke's unrelenting glare. "Find the outlaw. That's what we hired you to do. I don't want to hear your opinion. I want you to do your job."

Luke lifted slightly off the seat, hesitating when he saw Theo's face go pale. It took every ounce of willpower he could muster to keep from reaching across the desk and grabbing the man by the throat. Thoughts zipped through his mind in mere seconds. He wanted to tell Theo to find himself another bounty hunter, but that would mean they'd send someone else to go after Billie—maybe someone without a conscience. He wasn't sure why that mattered to him, but it did, and especially now that he'd hid her at his sister's house. "I'll do my job," he said between clenched teeth. "How about you do yours?"

A hint of color returned to Theo's face. "There's no reason for you to get so riled. We're both on the same side."

"Are we?" Luke sat back down.

"What are you implying?" Theo asked, his stare darkening.

"You find out what happened in the back room of

that bank," Luke said. "Who witnessed the killing? Why the sheriff wants to keep that the criminal's a woman a secret? You might not think any of that matters, but if I capture the wrong person, and it's a woman—you'll be the laughingstock of the agency for decades to come."

The last sentence hit home. Theo stared without blinking. The man's mind had to be buzzing like a hornet's nest.

Luke stood up. "I'll be back in a few days. Tell me what you find out. I'm going to Justice City to visit Sheriff McGregor."

The second he stepped outside the door, Laurence Magellan greeted him with a pointed nose, beady black eyes, and almost nonexistent lips. The man looked like a possum, except he used his pen and the press to bite instead of sharp teeth.

"So, I see you've come home empty-handed," Laurence said. "That won't be much of a story."

Luke shook his head. "I don't have time for your jabs today, Laurence. Unlike you, I've got a real job."

"Publishing a newspaper and exposing the cruelty of mankind is my job."

"So you've said." Luke moved toward his horse, unwrapping the reins from the hitching post. "You forgot making up lies to support your point of view."

Laurence lifted his nose. "I do no such thing."

Luke grabbed the saddle horn, stuck his foot in the stirrup, and pulled up into the creaking leather saddle. "What do you want?"

"I heard a rumor I thought might interest you."

Luke paused. Was he being baited? It was hard to tell. Since he'd fallen for Laurence's trickery before, he'd wait for more.

"I hear that someone by the name of Clovis Caldwell is sending a posse out to meet you. He seems to think you're conspiring with another someone who took gold that belongs to his bank."

Luke tried to keep his fingers from twitching as blood rushed through his extremities. He had not expected to hear the name Clovis Caldwell from Laurence's lips. Was Caldwell trying to do to him what he intended to do to McGregor—come at him with a quick right punch that left him confused and scrambling? If so, he'd have to do better than that. This wasn't his first time to encounter double-crossing liars. "Who gave you that bit of news?"

Laurence glanced about, obviously checking for anyone within hearing distance. "I can't say where I got the message, but lawmen talk. Our newest sheriff has a dubious background. I think he may be friends with Sheriff McGregor, who is an associate of Clovis Caldwell. At least that's the rumor I hear."

A faint breeze sifted down the dusty streets, stirring up sand and grit before calming down.

Several people strolled about with little concern for their conversation. A man and a woman walked along the wooden planks, entering the General Store along with three small children. Another man wobbled from the saloon doors and out onto the street. An older gentleman with a slight bend to his gait moved toward the bank.

Nothing unusual, but at the same time, something felt eerily wrong.

Luke searched the street and the tops of the buildings. Nothing. His danger sense prickled. "You seem to know quite a bit," Luke finally said. "But do you know the truth?"

Laurence shrugged. "The truth has a way of coming out in the end."

"I thought you wanted me dead," Luke said. "Why would you warn me?"

"Who said I wanted you dead?" A look of offense crossed Laurence's thin, angular face. "I only want you to find a new way of making a living. Bringing in criminals, many of whom are forced into crime by life circumstances, is beneath you."

"What's your solution? Let them run rampant? Steal and kill at their leisure with no consequences?"

"No. But at least find out why the poor souls chose a life of crime. Bringing someone in dead doesn't allow for rehabilitation."

"I never killed anyone, and you know it."

"But one day you will, and then what?"

"Look, we have opposing viewpoints, Laurence, but right now, I've got more on my mind than a debate with you. If I understand you right, this Caldwell person wants me dead. Probably because he thinks I know the truth." Luke's annoyance with Billie resurfaced. Why hadn't she told him everything? Now he was at a disadvantage—not knowing everything but people willing to kill him because they suspected differently.

"What truth?" Laurence asked.

Luke resisted the urge to grin. He could almost see Laurence salivate. No way would he tell a newspaper publisher anything. Not yet, anyway. "Thanks for the warning." Luke gave his horse a slight flick of the reins and the animal moved away.

"I don't want to write your obituary, Luke," Laurence called out. "At least, not yet."

"You won't," he answered, hoping it sounded confident.

How had everything fallen apart so quickly? Once again, he found himself mixed up in something that had nothing to do with him. Now he was in jeopardy, right along with Billie. He needed to find Sheriff McGregor. He only hoped he made it to the man alive.

6

Billie ran her hand over the blue cotton fabric of the dress, delighting in the smoothness that caressed her skin. It felt good to wear clean, feminine clothes again. The bath had been a blessing from above. Her skin and scalp still tingled from the hard scrubbing, reminding her of the pleasure long after it ended. Slender fingers reached up, tracing the white lace collar that accented the V-shaped neckline. "Thank you, Abigail. I feel human again."

"The dress fits you well. Much better than it ever fit me. It belonged to my mother, and even though she's gone to be with the Lord, I couldn't do away with it. It was her Sunday dress and always made me think of the bluebonnets that covered the hillside in the spring as we traveled to and from church. It's yours now."

"Oh, thank you. Are you sure?" At Abigail's nod, Billie smiled. "I'll take good care of it." Now she would not be embarrassed as she made her way to the relatives in Arkansas. Perhaps she could sidestep Caldwell's men. They weren't expecting her to look like a lady. If only she could do something about her hair. It stood out like a shiny copper penny in the bright Texas sun.

Henry, Jr., slept soundly in his mother's arms. Abigail looked unusually tired and pale. Bluish circles formed half-moons under her eyes. Cheekbones protruded above sunken flesh.

"Would you like me to hold Henry for you?" Billie offered.

"He's almost asleep," Abigail said. "I'll rock him a few more minutes then put him in his cradle." A few more minutes turned into almost half an hour. Abigail placed him in his bed, tucking the covers around his tiny shoulders. She gave him a gentle pat, a smile lifting her lips. "He's better now. Just as I prayed."

"Yes, but you look worn out. Why don't you rest, and I'll make us supper?"

"I like that idea." Abigail stood in the doorway to her bedroom, her hand upon the frame. "I need a short nap." She went into the room and fell across the mattress with a muted thud.

Billie laid her palm across Abigail's forehead. "You're hot as a branding iron."

Abigail buried her face deeper into a pillow and then curled into a ball.

Now what?

Billie didn't know much about taking care of sick people. She decided to fix Abigail some chicken broth, slice an apple, cook up a few vegetables, put a damp rag on her forehead, and pray. That was the extent of her doctor training.

And what about Henry Jr.? Billie couldn't nurse him, and a sick woman couldn't nurse him either.

Maybe there was a wet nurse nearby. She'd take him there if she knew which direction to go. Abigail could tell her after she woke.

When Henry, Jr. began to whimper a couple of hours later, Abigail didn't flinch a single muscle.

Billie changed his flannel diaper then moved to the rocking chair. Within a few minutes, he was back asleep—delicate breaths sifted between petal-pink lips and puffy cheeks. Wisps of hair moved about his small head along with every rocking motion. A faint smile flitted across his lips, causing her heart to swell.

The sound of shuffling feet drew her gaze to the bedroom doorway.

Abigail stood, propped against the frame but looking as if she might fall over any second.

"For goodness sake, sit down before you hurt yourself."

"You sound like me." Abigail lowered onto the mattress. "I'm sick, Billie."

"What can I do to help?"

"There's nothing you can do for me, but little Henry—" Her hand fell across her forehead. "There's a widow who lives west of here, about an hour or so down the road. She has a goat. Take him there. She'll feed him. She helped me with my first little one."

"Your first little one?" Confusion caused Billie to stop rocking. There'd been no mention of another baby.

"A girl. My milk didn't come in good that time, but the widow—she knows how to keep everything clean, so the babies don't get sick. Take Henry to her.

Her house is the first one you'll come to, but you've got to keep your eyes open. The hills almost hide it." Abigail slumped down.

"Where is the little girl?"

"She died of pneumonia in the first winter," Abigail whispered in a groggy voice.

Billie couldn't let anything happen to Henry, Jr. Abigail had already buried one child. She couldn't bury another. That was too much for a momma's heart to bear. "What about you?" Billie asked.

"As long as I know Henry is OK, I'll be OK." She rolled onto her side. "The widow will want something for the milk. Take her some of my prickly pear honey. It's in a flask on the cabinet shelf."

Billie scurried about the cabin to make Abigail as comfortable as possible before she left. She heated the chicken broth then poured it in a bowl, placing it beside the bed with a spoon. Fresh, cool water was drawn from the well, and Billie set the bucket within easy reach. Last of all, she wet a cloth and placed it across Abigail's forehead. "Don't move while I'm gone. I'll be back soon."

Dear Lord, don't let anything happen to this woman. I can't take care of a baby. Not now.

Billie got in the saddle with Henry, Jr. and guided the horse down the road in a slow sway. The babe seemed to enjoy the rocking motion and slept soundly until a few minutes before she drew close to the widow's house. He wiggled and whimpered as the horse came to a halt.

The house was built into a clump of mesquite

trees, positioned back against a large rock partition and easily unnoticed if not for someone looking.

The widow walked out onto the porch almost as if expecting her arrival. She was a beautiful Hispanic woman with creamy brown skin wrinkled from hours in the sun. Her black hair was streaked with strands of silver. White teeth shone against her skin when she smiled. "You brought Henry, Jr., to see me. I wondered if anyone would visit. Who might you be?"

"A friend of the family. I'm Billie. Abigail sent me here to have you feed the little man."

"Is she having trouble with her milk again?"

"Not this time. She's got a fever and can't nurse him."

The baby's whimpering suddenly turned into a squall that pierced the skies.

The widow hurried over, taking him from Billie.

Relief washed over Billie, and she smiled her thanks as she slid from the horse and followed the widow inside.

Within minutes, the widow had a nursing cup filled with goat's milk. Between heaving shoulders and wet cheeks, Henry, Jr. slurped and sucked as if he'd never tasted anything so good. When he'd had his fill, the widow placed him on her shoulder and began to pat until he wiggled, stiffened, and let out a loud burp.

"Now your tummy will feel good, won't it," the widow whispered to the babe before turning back to Billie. "I can give you enough milk to last the day, but you'll need to come back tomorrow for more. Babies require fresh milk every day. Clabbered milk can hurt their insides, especially one trying to gain strength."

After a few more questions about Abigail's sickness, the widow drew a piece of tree bark from her cupboard. She wrapped it in a cloth and handed it to Billie. "This is black willow bark. I managed to barter with an Indian woman passing through the woods for a few pieces, but this is all that's left. Boil the wood then strain it into tea. It will reduce fever and make her more comfortable. There are several doses, so don't use it all at once. Tell her not to breastfeed for at least two days after she is well."

With the bark safely tucked away and the widow's instructions memorized, Billie headed back to check on Abigail. Henry, Jr. fell asleep once more, resting on her shoulder as she guided the horse with one hand back toward his home.

Funny how she'd thought she would already be on her way to Arkansas, yet here she was—caring for a woman who was supposed to care for her. Not that she minded. She was thankful to repay at least a portion of Abigail's kindness. She only hoped it was enough.

The sun shone high in the sky, blazing across Billie's alabaster skin. She was bound to freckle, something her mother always encouraged her to avoid. Most of the time, she gave little heed to such thoughts, finding freckles perfectly fine, even interesting.

Besides, she was too proud to worry about such trivial matters. Not that she'd done anything great, except guide the horse, but she'd managed to get Henry Jr. fed and medicine for Abigail, all within a few hours.

As she rounded the last bend before the cabin, a gasp erupted from her lips. She jerked the reins, causing her horse to dig its hooves into the dirt.

Abigail stood on the porch. Several men sat on horses, positioned in a semi-circle. Abigail was talking to them.

Caldwell's posse.

Billie had to hide. *But where?*

With trembling fingers and her heart racing, Billie guided the horse toward scrawny bushes near a boulder. It wasn't much concealment, but it was all she had.

How had they found her? Amongst the tangled mesquite and cacti they'd managed to track her from so many days ago?

Had Luke sent them to capture her and maybe get his hands on some of the reward? That thought did not stay. He would not put his sister and nephew in such danger.

Abigail held onto the porch railing, about to collapse.

What have I done? What have I brought upon this family? Billie wanted to scream. With rattled nerves and trembling flesh, she eased the horse deeper into the brush, peering out through a web of barren branches.

If the men shot Abigail, she couldn't live with herself. But how could she stop anything without putting Henry, Jr. in danger? Anguish filled her soul and tears seared her eyes.

Lord, help me...I don't know what to do.

Minutes passed, but she didn't dare move into the clearing. With so little cover, she would be easy to spot. Instead, she waited—speaking fervent prayers and ignoring the faint beads of sweat that trickled down her spine.

After a good hour, Billie led her horse out into the open, trusting the men had gone. They'd never ridden past her, but that wasn't a good sign.

No one stood outside. Hopefully, Abigail rested comfortably on the bed, and Caldwell's men had left for good. If they'd done anything to her friend, her heart would break into a million pieces. She didn't want to imagine—

Billie's heels nudged the horse's flanks, urging the mare toward the cabin with a slow trot. What if they'd taken Abigail? Or, what if she rode into an ambush? The posse would kill her with little concern for the babe in her arms.

Billie eased off the horse. Henry remained on her shoulder. She drew the bucket of milk from the saddle horn and retrieved the plant the widow sent to help Abigail. With cautious footsteps, she made her way inside the darkened cabin.

Abigail lay on the mattress.

Relief swept over Billie. Was her friend breathing? "Abigail," she whispered.

Nothing.

Billie placed Henry, Jr., in his cradle then hurried to her friend. A firm nudge didn't move the sick woman. "Abigail." Billie touched her forehead. Abigail was burning hot. But at least she was alive.

Billie moved to the stove, taking out a piece of the bark. She dipped water from the bucket at the side of the stove and heated it to boiling. Dropping the bark in the water, she waited as it turned dark and simmered. She strained the liquid as the widow instructed and then added a pinch of honey.

Billie sat beside Abigail on the mattress. "You have to sit up. You can't die on me. Little Henry needs his momma."

At the mention of Henry's name, Abigail's eyes half-opened.

Billie lifted her head and helped her sip the bark tea. Abigail resisted, but Billie was patient. "You have to drink it."

Abigail drank slow but finally pushed the almost empty cup away.

"I saw you talking to Caldwell's men," Billie said.

"Monsters."

"What did they say?"

"They knew Luke brought you here."

"How could they possibly—"

"I don't know. I'm guessing they tracked you here." She opened her eyes, frowning. "I told them you had doubled-back and headed toward—" Her mouth parted and she sucked in a deep breath of air before continuing. "Toward Mexico. The man who did the talking said they'd come back and skin me alive if I'd lied."

Billie's insides tightened into a hard ball. "Luke said I'd be safe here, but now you're in danger, too."

"I'm a good shot. You don't have to worry about

me."

Not if you can't lift your head.

Billie reached out, touching Abigail's forehead again. A slight sweat covered the woman's face. The fever was breaking. Billie took the damp rag and wet it once again with cold water, pressing it against her friend's temples then laying it across her forehead. "I think you'll make it after all."

"Because of you," Abigail said with a faint smile. "I don't know what I'd have done if I was alone."

"You'd have gotten on a horse or walked if you had to, but you'd have made it to the widow's place. You wouldn't have let yourself die. You'd have done something—for Henry, Jr's. sake."

She grinned. "Yeah. I would've." She moved a thick lock of hair away from her face. "In that way, maybe we're not so different."

"Not so different at all."

Abigail's hand rose then fell across the top of Billie's hand in a feather-like touch. "Want to tell me what happened? Why those men are after you?'

She hesitated.

"Seeing as how they threatened me with an unthinkable death, I think I should know."

If anyone deserved to know the truth, it was Abigail.

7

The town of Justice City was small—not nearly as alive as El Paso, but a decent size for a West Texas community. Luke reasoned it was due to the train depot on the edge of town, which was always good for business.

As he'd passed a rock schoolhouse, he figured that was where Billie had taught children up until a few weeks ago. It looked deserted now with the windows and door boarded up. There was something sad about the building, a desolation that he knew only recently claimed the structure.

In an odd way, the sight reminded him of her. He pictured her alive and vibrant as she once stood in front of the classroom and taught children their letters, but now, her very soul lay hidden behind a barricade of despair. There was no getting in without a heap of trouble and determination—neither of which he wanted to give.

There were only a couple of streets in Justice City, and he stayed on the main one, guiding his horse past buggies, pedestrians, and places of commerce. He spotted the bank—only feet away from the sheriff's office.

So, that was the crime scene...

Part of him wanted to go inside, but he sensed that wasn't the brightest idea. Maybe another time.

With a click of his tongue and the press of his boot heels, he guided the horse to the general store. He looped the reins over the hitching post then walked inside with a shuffle of boots and a casual demeanor.

A man stood behind the counter, staring at a ledger. A woman straightened several bolts of cloth that had fallen over on a nearby table. Both wore white aprons with the words Harris Family General Store embroidered in dark green letters.

There were only a couple of shoppers inside, milling about the food supplies. He pretended to be interested in a few items as he waited for the shoppers to pay for their goods and leave. If he'd learned anything while bounty hunting, it was that folks in the general store and the local diner heard all the town gossip. He made sure one of those places was his first stop in any town when looking for an outlaw.

"Good afternoon." Luke tipped his hat at the man behind the counter. "I'm Luke Lancaster. Are you the owner?"

The man offered up a friendly smile. "Hello, Mr. Lancaster. And yes, welcome to our store. My name is Drake Harris, and this is my wife, Molly. You must be new in town."

"Just passing through."

He closed the ledger, setting it aside. "How may we help you today?"

"I'd heard a rumor about your schoolteacher."

Luke dove right into the middle of the mess. He'd also learned over his years as a bounty hunter that such an abrupt approach caught people off guard and often uncovered more truth than two hours of friendly chatter. "Something to do with thieving and murdering. Thought you might fill me in on the details."

The man's face flushed. "Why do you want to know?"

"I work for the Littleton and Clark Detective Agency. We've been hired by the Justice City Bank's insurance company to recover the outlaw and, hopefully, the stolen property. The bank has submitted a rather large claim and, as you might imagine, the insurance company isn't ready to pay until there's some form of resolution. That's why I'm here."

"That's all well and good." The man lifted his chin. "But I can't help you."

Luke shifted his stare toward Molly, who quickly turned away, eyeing the cloth as if she'd never seen taffeta before. A faint pink hue colored her cheeks. He could tell by the set of her jaw and trembling of her fingers that she had something to say and wanted to say it.

"The poster says dead or alive," Luke continued. "What'd a woman do to deserve death? Has she had a fair trial?"

"No." Beads of sweat dotted the store owner's forehead. "And she won't." He grabbed a duster behind the counter and began whipping it across the wooden top. "You best get on down the road, mister.

For your own safety."

"I intend to get to the truth," Luke stated with finality.

"That's not likely," the man countered.

Luke frowned.

Drake's eyes darted to the door then back again. "Clovis Caldwell's posse is looking for her, too. If they find her first—" The man stopped speaking, pressing his lips together.

Luke wasn't ready to quit poking around. "I understand she murdered a local man?"

"Billie Jo wouldn't hurt an ant!" The woman snapped, drawing their attention.

"Molly!" Drake pleaded, fear in his eyes. He turned toward Luke. "Mister, I need you to get outta here. You'll not cause me any trouble. I won't have it."

Molly whirled about, her petticoat slapping against her ankles as she headed toward the rear of the building, mumbling under her breath.

Luke nodded. He'd done enough damage here. Besides, he'd found out two important facts: the town's people were afraid to talk, and not everyone believed Billie was guilty. "Sorry to bother you," Luke said, turning to walk out the door. A noise came from the alley a few feet away. Instinctively, his hand lifted to his holstered gun.

"Pssst!" The sound came again.

Molly stuck her head out from behind a rear wall just enough to catch his attention and then disappeared.

His heart raced. He tried to appear nonchalant as

he strode around the side of the building, but every fiber in his body crawled with danger.

"Did anyone see you?" she asked with a whisper, her face pale.

He gave a quick glance over his shoulder. "No. I don't think so."

Molly reached up, digging her fingers into his arm with a vicious grip that accented the depth of her fear. "Are you trying to get yourself killed? When Clovis finds out you're snooping around, you'll be murdered, just like Malcolm."

"Malcolm?"

"The bank clerk who got shot in the head. Billie worked part-time, after school, for the bank. She and Malcolm worked together in the back room. Only most folks don't think it happened like Clovis says. Billie is my friend. She'd never shoot anyone, and certainly not over gold. I've known her my whole life." Her head snapped back and forth as she glanced about the alley. "People think Malcolm found out that Clovis was stealing from his own customers a little at a time so no one would notice, and Malcolm told Billie."

"If that's what people think, why hasn't anyone come forward and said so?" Restraint had returned and a certain calmness that defied the heightened situation. That's what made him good at his job. He was able to get himself under control quicker than most—even in dire circumstances. "Why hasn't anyone told Sheriff McGregor or someone else in law enforcement about their suspicions?"

"Clovis owns Sheriff McGregor." Dampness filled

her eyes. "Don't tell a soul we talked, or I'll end up in the bottom of a well with a cracked skull." Once more, her gaze darted from one end of the alley to the other. "Drake will come looking for me any second. I've got to get back inside. If you're here to help Billie, I'm glad, but be careful. You don't know who you're messing with."

"I can take care of myself," he said with quiet confidence.

"Maybe you can and maybe you just think you can," Molly said. "But at least I'll know I tried to warn you. That's all I can do…"

~*~

"So, you and Malcolm were friends." Abigail held Henry in her arms, giving him a drink of the goat's milk. Though her face still appeared ashen, at least her fever was at bay, and she'd had plenty of water—easing the dizzy spells.

Melancholy swept through Billie for the kind, older gentleman who never wavered in his faith, despite a blow that would cause other believers to crumble. She missed their talks on the Scriptures and how joy would shine in his eyes when he mentioned his wife of twenty years.

"Malcolm lost his entire family in a flood less than a year earlier," Billie said. "He took a job at the bank—more as a way to occupy his mind than the pay. He'd reconcile the day's accounts, and I worked at the bank after school. I'd file the paperwork. Over time, we naturally got to know one another. Then when Malcolm noticed several past deposits had been altered, he knew someone was stealing from the miners. No one had access to the vault except Malcolm and Clovis. Malcolm and I went together and told Sheriff McGregor, who said he would come by to see for himself."

"Who then showed up with Caldwell?"

"Yes. Intent on killing us both and making Sheriff McGregor out to be the hero for catching two gold thieves. But I messed up their plans. Somehow, by a miracle, McGregor stumbled over Malcolm's foot and shot a hole through the ceiling. But I got away."

"And now, they need you dead to protect themselves," Abigail said, sitting in the rocker and placing Henry on her shoulder. The baby whimpered a couple of times before drawing up his legs and growing quiet.

"I'm the only one alive who knows their secret."

"As much as I hate to say it, maybe you should go to Arkansas. Any place, really. As long as they can't find you."

"I'm amazed I'm still alive," Billie said. "Every day I think this is my last day, but somehow, I'm still here."

Abigail began to pat the baby on the back, anxiety hovering over her gaze like a dark storm cloud. "Does Luke know any of this?"

Billie fumbled with the sleeve of her dress. An awkwardness settled between her and Abigail. She moved her hand to her stomach. Why did the mere mention of the man's name cause her insides to quiver?

"No. Luke only knows Caldwell's posse is trying to kill me and anyone else who gets in their way." She paused, giving Abigail a hard stare. "You're not safe with me here. No one is safe with me around."

"I already got a taste of that. I'd love for you to stay and help me with Henry and the farm. But for your own sake, you need to go. It'll be best for you."

And for us. Abigail would never say the words, but she had a baby to consider and harboring a wanted criminal was a good way to bring trouble no one in their right mind would want.

Billie focused out the window and the dusty earth on the other side of the pane. "I'll leave soon. When I know you're able to take care of yourself and little Henry."

"I think you'd be smart to wait for Luke and let him go with you," Abigail said, surprising Billie with the thought. "He'll get you where you're going in one piece."

The thought only made her more annoyed and more determined not to wait, even though her heart whispered something else. "Who knows when Luke might return, or if he will. I can't make my plans around him."

Abigail bowed her head then looked back up with a faint smile. "When the time is right, I trust you'll do the right thing."

Guilt slid over Billie's shoulders like a cold wind. She needed to get away from Texas as soon as she could. Waiting on Luke to wander back when it suited him was not part of her plans.

She'd miss Abigail's friendship and baby Henry's sweet face. But for today, she'd enjoy their company, keep doctoring her friend, and feeding the little man. Unless Luke happened to show up in the next few days, she'd seen the last of him.

8

"Sheriff McGregor?" Luke's form filled the doorway to the sheriff's office, blocking most of the sun except for what seeped in around his muscular frame.

"Maybe..." A man stood near the stove, pouring a cup of coffee. "Who's asking?"

The man was not at all what Luke expected from a sheriff. There wasn't anything intimidating or authoritative about the man's presence. He was pale in complexion with sandy-brown hair, a recessed chin, and hazel eyes that somehow felt mocking. He was small in stature with a gun holster that draped loose across thin, almost boyish hips. A blade of wheat or barley rolled about his lips, his tongue moving it about his mouth with ease.

But looks could deceive. Luke had not stayed alive this long by lowering his guard. "Luke Lancaster with Littleton and Clark Detective Agency from El Paso, Texas. I'm a recovery specialist, hired on behalf of Justice City Bank by their insurance company."

"And?" The man stirred a spoon full of sugar about his cup with a steady hand. The man obviously wasn't surprised to hear his name.

"And, I'm looking to find out who stole the gold from the bank's vault. Are you the sheriff?"

"Yep, and you're a little behind. I already gave the thief's name and description to your agency."

Luke intended to play it cool but not for long. "I think there may be some confusion over who actually took the gold and killed the bank clerk." He dipped his chin downward and raised a brow. "Maybe if we shared notes..."

If what Molly said was true, Sheriff McGregor knew that Clovis Caldwell meant to kill him. And right now, they were playing chess, though neither knew the other person's next move.

McGregor plopped down in a chair, pointing Luke toward the empty chair opposite him. Not once did his gaze leave Luke. A table rested between them, probably where he ate his meals and shuffled papers.

A separate room jutted off the main room, showing a portion of a large jail cell. It looked as if it had been added on rather than being part of the original structure. "Any prisoners back there?"

The sheriff leaned back in his chair, cocking his head in arrogance. "Why're you asking?"

"Because this is a private conversation."

"No prisoners yet," he said. "I've got two cells ready and waiting. 'Course, prisoners don't stay around here long. They either die a mysterious death or disappear during the night." A slight twitch moved over his upper lip as he grinned. "Funny how things like that happen."

Luke wasn't amused. Coldness seeped from his

flesh into his bones. "What can you tell me about the bank robbery that cost a clerk his life?"

"Not much," Sheriff McGregor said, shifting his weight then continuing without giving him a chance to respond. "Don't plan on getting involved." He tapped his fingers on the table, not the least anxious. "Leaving that one to the insurance company and the professionals to sort out."

Luke's eyes narrowed. "But you're the one who submitted the criminal report. Right?"

Mocking eyes turned sinister, dripping with evil intent. "So?"

Luke remembered the time he watched a buffalo stomp a young brave to death. He'd only been eight or nine years old when his father took him on his first buffalo hunt. They'd cornered the herd and thought they'd have an easy go of it until one of the animals turned and barreled toward a brave, knocking his horse over then stomping him to death before anyone could stop him.

The memory of the brave's screams and the horrible crunching of bones against hooves had left a horrible scar in Luke's memory. The worst part of it all was when the bull finished stomping on him, it lifted his head and looked right at Luke—as if he were next.

A spear pierced the beast's lungs and ended the bull's rage, but Luke would never forget the look in its eyes that cold winter day. Merciless. Barbaric. Empty. That was the same look he saw when he met McGregor's gaze—a bloodthirsty stare that made him question if the man even had a soul.

"Why'd you hide from the agency the fact that the suspect was a woman? You led everyone to think Billie was a man. Was it so they'd shoot first then ask questions later?"

McGregor gave a quick laugh. "Guess our friendly conversation is over."

"It was over the second your boss decided to have me killed."

"What boss?"

"Clovis Caldwell," Luke said without flinching. Something on the inside of him had started to take root—a calmness that would keep his mind focused. His heartbeat slowed. "I know what happened in the backroom of that bank with Malcolm and Billie."

"Since you're so smart—" The sheriff's upper lip twitched again. "Why don't you tell me?"

"I don't have to tell you. You were there. You murdered Malcolm." Luke was bluffing—speaking rumors as if they were truth. From the vicious expression that erupted on the sheriff's face, he'd hit pay dirt. "You would've killed Billie, too, but she escaped."

McGregor shook his head, rubbing his fingers along his chin. The man seethed with a contempt that Luke could feel. "Seems to me you're letting your affections for Billie Jo blind you to the truth. That means you know where she is. Have you told your employer that you're derelict in your duty, or should I tell him?"

"If anyone has abandoned their oath," Luke began. "It's you."

"Is that right?" The sheriff moved his right hand ever so slightly, bending his elbow.

"Don't even think about it," Luke said. "I can take you on your best day."

Sheriff McGregor relaxed his right hand, but Luke could tell by his deathly stare that he'd almost reached his breaking point—that maybe Luke had pushed him too far.

"I didn't come here to kill you," Luke said. "I'd already done it if that was the plan. I came here to give you a message for Caldwell."

The sheriff stared at him without speaking.

"Tell him he'd better leave Billie alone."

"Or what?"

"Or he'll be the one hunted."

Sheriff McGregor stared.

Luke rose from the chair, turned around, and walked out the door—not once looking back but feeling pure hatred stabbing him in the back.

~*~

Billie squinted into the early sun looking at the cabin from a good hundred yards away. Even at that distance, she could see Abigail's body in a heap of burgundy cloth on the front porch.

No!

Her heart pounded. She leaned forward, flicking the reins and holding tight as her horse took off on a full run. Had Caldwell's men killed Abigail?

Please, God. Let her be alive!

Could she have fainted? When Billie left this morning, Abigail had been fine. She'd insisted she could watch Henry, Jr. Against her better judgment, Billie had agreed. Without having to hold a baby the entire way, she could make the trip back and forth in half the time. What a dreadful mistake. One more to add to her growing list.

Billie's mind scrambled for answers before she made it to her friend. The baby's wailing sounded inside the house as she drew closer. If Abigail were alive, she would never let Henry, Jr., cry. Her gaze darted about as she envisioned Caldwell's men coming out of the mesquite trees and boulders with guns blazing, but no such thing happened.

Her feet landed on the ground before her horse completely stopped. She bumped the bucket of goat's milk, sloshing a fair amount onto the dirt but not caring as she ran up the steps.

Billie fell on her knees beside Abigail, checking her wrist for a pulse. The woman's cheeks shone scarlet, but the rest of her glistened a damp, pasty white. She was alive but limp and blazing hot. Her fever had returned with a vengeance.

Billie grabbed Abigail by the arms and pulled her through the cabin door, her wounded shoulder screaming in agony at the exertion. She glanced down, expecting to see blood trickling down her arm, but the bandage held.

Once inside, she lifted Abigail onto the bed then scurried outside to the water pump to wet a rag with fresh water. She lay the cloth across Abigail's forehead, pressing the coolness into her pores. Abigail tried to push her hand away, but Billie wasn't having it.

Billie feared for her friend's life. She lit the stove and dropped the last of the black willow bark into the water to boil. Then she picked up little Henry and held him close.

Sobs wracked his tiny body, but her comforting softened his cries. She hurried outside, wrapping her fingers around the metal handle of the bucket and lifting it from the saddle horn. Goat's milk sloshed against the side, but, thankfully, no more spilled. Henry, Jr., seemed to sense what was coming and began to fuss, wiggling about like a wet cat.

"Hold still, little man. I don't want to drop you." She sat down at the foot of the mattress where Abigail lay and let him suck the nursing cup holding the goat's milk. He drank as if he'd gone days instead of a few hours without nourishment, barely stopping to take a breath.

As soon as he was satisfied, she placed him in the cradle and then poured the tea.

Abigail resisted. She coughed and sputtered at first then took the next swallows without protest.

Billie tipped the rest of the drink down her throat with a steady but slow hand.

Within half an hour, Abigail opened her eyes and a healthy color rested upon her cheeks.

"I thought you were dead." Now that her friend was safe, exhaustion from fear and exertion set in. "How'd you get out there on that porch?"

"I don't know," Abigail mumbled. "Last thing I

remember was wanting to get some milk for baby Henry. He was complaining something awful. I changed his diaper, and that's all I can recall. I think I may have had fever sickness."

"You had something. About scared the life out of me."

"I'm sorry. I keep thinking I'm getting better, and then—" She shrugged.

Billie prepared some soup, poured it into a bowl, and placed it in Abigail's hands. She set a plate with a slice of buttered bread and a whole apple on the table. "Well, that settles that."

"What settles what?" Abigail asked.

"I can't leave this place until someone else comes to stay with you or until I'm certain you're well enough to care for the baby. If this happens again, I don't know if you'd make it."

"I'm sorry." Abigail looked at her with regret.

"When will your husband be back?"

"Soon," Abigail said, her gaze shifting to the bowl of soup. "He sells all his wares before he returns." She rolled the spoon about the liquid. "I know it's not safe for you here."

"Or you," Billie reminded her. "Not as long as I'm here."

"Maybe little Henry and I can go to the widow's house and wait there for Henry. That way, you can leave before those men come back."

Billie felt compassion swell within her heart. There was no room in the widow's cabin. She'd seen the inside and it was only half the size of Abigail's home, if that. It just wouldn't do. "Little Henry is used to it here, and he's doing better. I don't think it would be wise to move him around."

"Yes, but you need to go. Those men will kill you."

Billie's gaze moved from Abigail's sweet expression to the window—drawn by an image that made her insides recoil. A posse of five or so men headed their way. She could see their figures tall in the saddle with dust from the hooves of horses surrounding them like an ominous cloud. The sun shone behind them, making them all appear like black stick figures. She closed her eyes. This could not be happening. "God, *why*?"

"Why what?" Abigail asked, sitting up on her elbows to see out the window.

"They're back," Billie said, her throat tightening. "Caldwell's men."

"You've got to hide," Abigail exclaimed. "Get to the root cellar. And be quick about it."

"No." Billie stood up with fists clenched at her side, her chin hard, and her stare unbending. "I'm tired of hiding. I'm staying right where I'm at."

9

The rush of blood pushed through Billie's being and stirred her determination.

"Don't be a ninny!" Abigail sat up slowly, sliding her legs over the edge of the mattress. "You'll get us all killed. Go out back and hide in the root cellar."

There was not an ounce of her that wanted to hide anywhere. She was tired of feeling like a hunted animal—always running but never getting away. "No. I'm tired of hiding."

Anguish pressed into Abigail's forehead. "Then do it for my sake and little Henry's sake."

Billie's expression twisted in turmoil. Abigail's words were a slap of reality across the face. "Did you forget? These men threatened to skin you alive. I'd never forgive myself if anything—"

"I know how to handle these men," she interrupted with bold assurance that showed in the set of her jaw. "I used to bounty hunt with Luke. If I stay calm, I can say the right words that'll send them down the road. But if I have to worry about you, I'll trip over my tongue, and only the good Lord knows what I might say."

Billie had never heard of a brother and sister

bounty team. How far her world had tipped from her simple life as a teacher—a teacher who enjoyed Sundays with family and weekly dinners at the homes of her students.

Only a couple of weeks ago, the biggest excitement she'd had was buying a piece of taffy from the general store. Now, she was hiding on the outskirts of the desert—protected by bounty hunters and tracked by gunmen eager to make a few dollars off her life.

"Now, git," Abigail ordered, rising from the bed with a stiff spine and clenched fist.

Billie hurried out the door, still not convinced she was doing the right thing. She grabbed a gun on the way out, determined to come out of hiding if she heard a single shot. She was not letting another friend die while doing nothing. She slid inside the root cellar, cracking the door to hear the conversation.

Abigail stood on the porch only feet away, probably as weak as a newborn foal.

At least Billie had fed her and made her fever break.

"Morning," Abigail said. Her voice sounded strong and clear.

"Morning, ma'am," a man spoke. "Had any visitors in your part of the country?"

"Not lately," Abigail said. "Who are you looking for?"

"A murderer," he answered. "With a high price tag."

"Who got murdered?" Abigail asked.

The men at the porch could not be the same group

who'd come around before. How many regiments had Clovis sent after her? She was afraid to know.

"An elderly bank teller," the man said. "Simply trying to do his job."

"That's horrible," Abigail's voice rose.

"Notice any missing food or other items from around your property?"

"No. We don't have much, but it's all here."

"Mind if we look around?"

"Not at all," Abigail said, sounding like she meant it.

Billie drew the door to the root cellar closed. The structure consisted of stone and wood across the front with a mound of cool dirt built into the hillside to keep the contents fresh. She could not stand up entirely but maneuvered about slightly hunched over. A small supply of potatoes lay in a basket near the door. Behind the potatoes sat a basket of apples given to the family by a neighbor. Several baskets of wood sat stacked to the ceiling in small enough bundles for Abigail to carry into the house as needed. Deeper into the cellar were the turnips, onions, and carrots, buried and waiting to be plucked out for the next meal. A shelf had been built which held several jars of blackberry jam. A slab of salt-cured ham hung from the ceiling.

Thinking quick, Billie moved the baskets holding the wood to the front of the entrance, forming a semi-shield she could hide behind by pressing herself against the dirt wall. The men might search the yard, too, and she wanted to be hidden in case anyone ventured inside.

Confident she'd made herself as invisible as possible, Billie crouched down behind the barrier and waited. Five minutes later, her eyes adjusted to the darkness, but her knees and back ached. The hip she thought had healed let her know it still had a ways to go. At least it was semi-cool where she hid, and she was alive. She prayed that no one would open the door—that it would remain invisible to the searchers.

A large spider moved across the floor in slow motion. She cringed, hoping there were no other insects or varmints nearby. The good Lord knew she would scream if a mouse or snake came near her.

She heard the muted sound of men's voices then a single pair of footsteps nearing. She pressed herself against the wall—her breath ragged and heartbeat jumping. *Lord, let them only peek inside and not dare enter. Please, Lord.* Seconds later, the voices disappeared along with the sound of footsteps. Still, she remained frozen in place—not trusting who might wait on the other side of the door.

Another ten minutes later and the door creaked open, light shining a brilliant beam into the cool darkness. Billie's stomach balled into an instant knot, and her heart felt as if it might stop in mid-beat. Her fingers tightened upon the gun.

"Billie?" Abigail called.

Billie's shoulders rolled forward in relief. Her chin dropped.

"Come out of there. They're gone."

~*~

Luke walked with Theo toward a diner for a cup of coffee and breakfast.

Theo scratched his head and then raked his chin with knuckles dotted by silvery-blond hair. "So, you think McGregor and Caldwell set this whole thing up?"

"That's exactly what I think," Luke said.

The café faced the street. Wide windowpanes let passersby see inside.

"And I'm not the only one who thinks it. I talked to a couple at the general store—"

"Will they offer a statement?"

"Not likely. From what I heard, no one will speak out against Caldwell or McGregor. They're afraid what happened to Malcolm will happen to them." Luke scanned the dining room.

It was later in the morning, and most of the breakfast crowd had cleared out. Twenty people sat inside, though there was space for a good twenty more.

A young waitress greeted them with a smile. She was the only one taking care of the room and a familiar face to both men. "Good morning, gentlemen. Have a seat. I'll be right there."

Luke chose a table that allowed him to keep watch over the street. He wasn't sure what he was watching for, but he'd know it when he saw it.

"You think someone is tailing you?" Theo asked, appearing much more relaxed than when they'd met a few days earlier. Perhaps because he'd left the confines of the office and overeager ears?

"I'm sure of it."

"Caldwell?"

"Maybe, but I don't think so." He glanced up as the waitress neared with two cups of black coffee in hand. "Whoever it is, they know what they're doing."

The waitress's perky voice broke the tension. "What would you like for breakfast? We have the usual plus the best apple pie on this side of the Jordan River."

Luke smiled at her before speaking. "I'll take buttered biscuits and gravy."

"Make that two."

She disappeared after a quick bob and twirl.

"It's not one of ours following you, if that's what you're thinking," Theo said. "You're the only one we've got on the case. We trust you to handle it."

"I think it's Comanche. My native brothers aren't happy with me."

"Because …?"

Luke figured he'd already stepped in this far. Might as well wade in deeper. "Two reasons. I chose a different life than what they live. Then I made matters worse by refusing to marry into the tribe. It was a double 'no, thank you' to all they hold dear."

Theo shrugged. "So, marry into the tribe. It'll keep the peace. Besides, the Comanche allow you several wives. Right? You can always marry the one you love later."

Luke shook his head, wondering why he'd thought it was a good idea to spend more time with

Theo. "Marriage is a covenant between one man and one woman."

"Ah, yes." Theo's finger twirled around his coffee cup. "I forget your file said a Christian woman raised you."

"Not just any Christian woman. My mother. She knew the Bible inside and out. There was never a more devout believer."

He cocked his head. "And yet, here you are. Bounty hunting."

"What does that have to do with anything?" Luke grumbled.

"Seems like an odd combination." Theo shrugged. "That's all."

"It's not so odd. My mother's faith has kept me from killing more than once."

"Your mother's faith," Theo repeated. "Not your own?"

A lone man walked by the window in slow motion, his gaze on them.

Luke tensed until the man disappeared. Even then, the tightness in his chest remained—a physical reminder that another person wanted him dead. He needed to get out of town and back into the wilderness where he had the upper hand. Right now, he felt like a sitting target. He took a slow sip of coffee, keeping alert. "So, what will you do about Sheriff McGregor?"

"I'll get some men on it. I may send someone in undercover to work for him. I'll have to go through proper channels and get approval from the governor, but I'll make something happen. You can count on it."

Luke wished that was true. Theo was growing on him, but the man still didn't have his trust. As the office director and the one handling the case, Theo should've known that the outlaw was a woman. Of course, he hadn't any reason to check it out, but if his men had done due diligence and talked to people around Justice City, they'd have known the truth. Instead, they went by what the sheriff said—a sheriff who appeared greedy for ill-gotten gain.

Almost every criminal case he handled could be traced back to the love of money. He was thankful his mother had taught him to find contentment in simple pleasures rather than silver and gold: a beautiful sunset, the laughter of a child, the sound of an owl, the taste of wild plums. And the love of family. She'd taught him what mattered. All the other things were fine but fleeting—never held with a closed fist. His native family had taught him that, too.

The waitress appeared, carrying both plates. "Here you go. Enjoy."

Warm biscuits lay in a blanket of thick, pepper-speckled white gravy. A small serving of baked apple with a dash of cinnamon served as an after-meal treat.

Theo gave her a quick 'thank you' smile then cut into his biscuit. "What you need to do is lay low for a few weeks. Give me time to get all the pieces in place. Then let's see what we can find out about McGregor and Caldwell."

"A few weeks?" Luke's elbows bit into the top of the table. "What am I supposed to do for a few weeks?"

"I'll give you money if that's why you're bothered. You've already done more investigating into the crime than our usual investigators. I'd say you've earned it."

"I'm not worried about the money. I'm wondering what I'll do with that much time." Luke sliced into his own biscuit. "I'm not exactly the sit around and twiddle my thumbs type."

"You'll find something to occupy your interest." Amusement crinkled Theo's lips as he stifled laughter. "Maybe get married? Enjoy a nice teepee honeymoon..."

Luke glanced up, wanting to give him a hard glare but chuckling instead, glad to have a little relief. But he didn't dare let his guard down. Watch out. Remain alert. Be ready.

Anything could happen.

10

Abigail's sickness continued to come and go—sometimes lingering for hours and other times lingering for a day or two.

It hurt Billie to watch her friend suffer, but she continued to pray.

For several days and nights in a row, Abigail's fever soared then dropped. It never rose to the point of delirium again, but it kept her immobile, faint, and thirsty. If the fever wasn't hard enough, every day Abigail had to drain her swollen breasts to keep from drying up her supply for little Henry in the future. She literally cried over spilt milk that wasn't safe for her baby.

The next day started pleasant enough. There was no sign of fever, and Abigail even laughed at something silly Billie had said. There'd been no more visits by Caldwell's men, but that didn't bring peace of mind. That only meant the time was getting shorter before someone showed up again.

She wanted Abigail well so she could leave for Arkansas with a clear conscience. Every convicting thought inside her brain told her she was putting her friend and her baby in grave danger. Little Henry was thriving, despite or perhaps because of the goat's milk, and even began to coo. When he yawned, he opened his tiny mouth wide and squinted, melting her heart and causing her to long for motherhood and a child of her own.

If she survived, perhaps God would grant her such a beautiful gift. A husband and a passel of children. That was her heart's desire, but at this point, she dared not hope. She kept her mind focused on getting through one day at a time.

Several days went by with no sign of fever. A neighbor from a nearby town brought a letter from Abigail's husband, Henry. The neighbor did not stay long, saying he had other mail to take around.

Billie hid in Abigail's bedroom the entire time she visited with him, not wanting anyone besides the widow to know she existed. She longed to write a letter to her parents but feared it might give away far more than it would help. Besides, the more her parents knew about her comings and goings, the more their lives would be in jeopardy. Though it pained her to think of their suffering, it was for the best.

Abigail waved good-bye to the neighbor and then did a quick swirl about the small room, squealing in delight.

Billie laughed at the sight, not remembering a single time she'd been so excited to get a letter. The color in her friend's cheeks proclaimed what she already knew—Abigail was whole and well. She could leave for Arkansas. The thought left her melancholy instead of joyful. Part of her wanted to stay a while longer. The small cabin had grown comfortable. She'd become attached to Henry, Jr., and to Abigail. It was not safe or practical to remain. She had to go, but this time, she was leaving of her own free will.

Abigail tore open the envelope. She unfolded a single sheet of paper. "He says he's making his last delivery and will be home by the end of the week!"

"That's great news."

"You'll love my Henry," Abigail gushed, holding the letter to her bosom. "He's a gentleman with a big heart. He'll be so excited to see how well Henry, Jr., is doing, and I have you to thank for it."

Would Abigail say such a thing if Caldwell's men showed up with guns blazing? Billie prayed her friend could not see the worry in her gaze. "God has heard our cries and answered our prayers."

Abigail's hand dropped, the letter still held in her fingers. Her joy turned into a look of despondency, as if she'd lost something precious with no hope of getting it back. "You're leaving, aren't you? You'll not meet my Henry."

"I'm sorry, it's just—"

Abigail held her hands upward, palms out. "Please. Don't say anything. I'll bring in some wood. I'll return in a few minutes."

"Abigail—" Billie's heart dipped. She hated hurting her friend, but putting her in danger any longer than necessary overrode any other thoughts.

Abigail stood at the door. "I'll be fine. Just worry about yourself."

Billie said a silent prayer asking God to soothe her

soul.

~*~

A whistle, loud and long, shattered the tranquil evening.

"It's either my husband or my brother." Abigail's rocker slowed as Henry, Jr., grunted.

Billie stopped peeling potatoes, her pulse quickening.

Abigail rolled the babe onto her shoulder, rose from the rocking chair, and went to the door.

Billie set the potato and knife aside, wiping her hands on her apron. She untied the garment, and dropped it across a chair before joining Abigail outside.

Even from a distance, Billie recognized the broad shoulders, bronze skin, and coal-black hair. Her throat felt suddenly dry, as if she'd swallowed an old, dusty rag.

"Luke..." Abigail breathed, her words disappearing on the wind.

"What's he doing back here?" Billie asked.

"Coming to check on us, that's all." Abigail rose on her tiptoes, smiling and waving in excitement.

Luke's stallion broke into a gallop, closing the distance separating them in a matter of seconds. He pulled the horse to a stop before removing his hat and wiping a sweaty brow with the sleeve of his shirt. "Good evening, ladies. Think you might have rations to spare for a weary bounty hunter?"

His gaze took her in, but she couldn't decipher the flash in his eyes. He probably hoped she'd already left or been captured.

"Well, I don't know," Abigail said with a teasing tone. "We don't take much to strangers around these parts. Especially those who disappear during the night without so much as a good-bye."

"Better be careful what you say." He slid from his horse, a grin teasing the edges of his lips. "Or I might stick around for a month or two. Then we'd see how you like it." He kissed her on the cheek and then patted the baby. "Henry, Jr's., looking good. Finally filling out that saggy skin of his." He turned to Billie.

She willed her pulse to slow down. A knot wedged itself in her throat. She'd forgotten the power of his presence—so sure, so casual, and so very masculine. Even the smell of him drew the strength from her knees. And those eyes, dark and mysterious, dared her to dive in. She knew there was no excuse for such thoughts, but neither could she pretend they did not exist. Her hand quivered, and she grew annoyed at the betrayal. It was a relief to realize that Luke did not seem to notice or care.

"Good to see you alive."

"Yes." She looked away. "You, too."

"Let's get you inside," Abigail said. "Billie's cooking up some potatoes to go with our greens and cornbread."

~*~

Luke wished he'd mentally prepared to see Billie again. He'd pictured finding her as he'd left her—disguised in smelly men's clothing with her braided hair stuffed under a hat and barely able to get around. Instead, she looked every inch a woman and moved with such grace, it took his breath away. He'd known she was attractive, even beneath the trail dust and bravado, but there was something more—an inner beauty that he'd failed to see before. The smart part of him hoped she hadn't caught the gleam of admiration in his eyes.

Billie Jo was more than fair. He couldn't think of her as just Billie. He pictured her now in front of a classroom full of students. A few of the older boys would have a crush on her, but she'd probably know how to deflect their attention without destroying their ego.

She would most likely not be so delicate with him. If he even gave her a grin, she might give him a good scolding and remind him how he'd almost left her to die in a hail of bullets.

He dropped his hat on a peg. "How's your arm and hip?"

The smell of coffee and burning mesquite filled the air. The sound of potatoes bobbing about in boiling water kept the silence away.

Billie Jo looked as if she might bolt any second. "I'm well. Thanks to your sister." An undercurrent of disapproval lingered in her gaze. "Not sure how she learned to doctor like she did, but—"

"Our mother," he interrupted. "And our mother

learned from the natives."

"She learned well, then."

Awkwardness filled the space between them.

Only Abigail appeared unaffected as she held Henry, Jr., close and disappeared to the separate bedroom. Was she giving them time alone? If so, why?

Billie Jo ran palms down the front of her dress. "You're most likely hungry. I'll get you a plate ..."

"Before you do that...I talked to your friend, Molly. She believes you're innocent."

Her face went white. "You shouldn't have done that. You shouldn't have talked to Molly or anyone in Justice City."

"I thought you'd be glad to know someone believed in you."

"They'll kill her."

"No one saw us talking."

"Are you sure?" Her fingers quivered as they flitted across the lace accenting the dress's neckline. "If Sheriff McGregor or Caldwell—"

"Don't worry. I talked to McGregor, too."

"Heaven help me! Have you lost your mind?" She dropped into the dining table chair, her face even more pale. "They probably followed you here."

He leaned back, crossing his arms. "No one followed me here."

"These men are ruthless," she said with bitterness. "McGregor shot my friend in cold blood. Right in the head. I saw it and—" Tears filled her eyes.

He fought the urge to take her in his arms and comfort her. It would only earn him a good kick in the shin. "Molly told me. And I'm sorry. Real sorry."

"I need to get out of here," she said, shooting up from the seat. "I need to go to Arkansas. I should leave right away. Tonight. If Caldwell's posse returns—"

"Hold on a minute," Luke interrupted. He stepped toward her, his hands coming to rest on her shoulders. "Let's sit down and eat. Then I'll tell you what I've learned."

"Promise you won't try to stop me from leaving."

"You can go whenever and wherever you want."

Billie Jo eyed him with suspicion. "It's for your family's safety."

"Would it surprise you if I agreed with your decision?"

"Yes…"

"Texas is too hot for you right now. You need to get far away. And I think I can help you do that."

"How can you help *me*?"

"I'm coming with you," he said, picking up a piece of bread. "That's how."

11

The dim light from the kerosene lamp brought a yellow-gold glow to the room.

Luke rose from the rocking chair, handing off a sleeping Henry, Jr., to his mother.

Billie Jo finished drying the dishes.

He went to the door.

"You sleep well," Abigail said.

"I will." His gaze shifted toward Billie Jo. "Good night."

"Good night."

The door closed. The sound of his boots moved from the wooden porch and disappeared into the night.

Abigail began to sing to her baby. It was a sweet tune that caused Billie's eyes to grow heavy, but she continued to sweep the floor—the final touch to a clean cabin.

A few seconds into the song and Abigail suddenly stopped singing. "My brother is like a wounded eagle."

Billie's brows pinched together. "How's that?"

"I guess I can tell you now since you practically saved my life."

Billie sat down on the mattress, only a few feet away from the rocking chair. "Tell me what?"

"I never thought he'd help another soul. He hasn't been the same since that girl came here." Abigail repositioned the baby. "He blames himself for our mother's death."

Billie's insides knotted. She knew that feeling. It was her fault her friend was dead, and she hated it. "Why? What happened?"

"Well..." Abigail didn't hide the pain that resided within her gaze. "There was a young woman from our father's tribe, no more than sixteen years old. She fell down the side of a steep hill and was left to die. Luke found her and brought her to our mother for healing. Our mother gave her food, water, and bandaged her wounds. Most instances, that's a good thing." Baby Henry began to squirm, so she started to rock him once more. "Luke loved Momma more than anyone in the whole world. I know it sounds silly, but there were times I was jealous." She laughed, a soft delicate sound that assured Billie that her love far outweighed any other emotions. "In her later years, Momma's legs stopped working right, and she couldn't get around well, but she still made do. Except the young woman wasn't in her right mind. I'd gone to check on them when—" Abigail's eyes misted over. "One of neighbors told me the girl burned the house down, with our mother asleep inside and then ran away."

"No..." Anguish filled Billie's lungs. "Why?"

"Luke found out later that the young woman was put out of the village because she was sick in the head—she kept setting fire to everything. Her people couldn't help her, so they banished her. But by the time we learned this truth, it was too late to save our mother."

Billie's lungs ached from the weight of Abigail's words. What a cruel twist of fate—trying to help someone only to have them murder the person one loved.

"Luke hasn't forgiven himself. Or God." She stood up, moving to the doorway with the babe in her arms. "I'm going to sleep. Remember my brother in your prayers. And Henry, Sr., too. Pray he returns safely and soon."

Billie wasn't the only one to carry the heavy burden of guilt upon her shoulders.

Luke had his own heartache to bear.

Their wounds were more similar than either knew.

~*~

Billie reached up, placing an affectionate kiss upon Abigail's cheek and then little Henry's brow. This was the right thing to do, but doubts remained. "You sure you'll be all right?"

The morning sun broke across the horizon in a blaze of yellow and orange. Blue skies sprawled across the heavens with scattered white clouds proclaiming the magnificence of the day before it fully arrived.

"I'll be fine," Abigail assured her. "I'll miss you, but Henry, Sr., will be here by the end of the week. We're all healthy and happy, so you don't need to concern yourself with us. Just worry about yourself. You're the one with a price on your head."

"I'll miss you something fierce," Billie said, giving her a firm hug. Heat burned her eyes. "Please tell me I'll see you again."

"I pray so," Abigail said. "Good Lord willing." She turned a hopeful expression toward her brother. "You take good care of her, you hear?"

Billie grabbed the saddle horn and pulled up onto the horse, repositioning her dress over her pantaloons to maintain some sense of modesty. There would be no riding sidesaddle like a proper lady. Luke had already delivered firm instructions. They'd travel hard and fast, and she didn't want to fall off trying to keep up.

Billie's gaze rested upon the man in front of her. He sat tall in the saddle with a silent but sure confidence. She was thankful to have him join her. Now she might make it to Arkansas alive. Once there, he'd be on his own getting back, but a man like Luke would have no trouble traveling alone. He knew how to hunt, track, and how to stay hidden.

He looked at her and unnerved her with that glance. "Ready?"

She nodded, keeping her lips pressed together and spine straight. She glanced back once more, closing her eyelids tight to keep the tears away then looked toward Luke.

He snapped the reins and sent his horse into a gallop. She did the same.

They stopped several hours later near a stream to refresh the horses and eat. Abigail had wrapped up some fried chicken and placed it in a bag for today's meal. After that, it'd be pemmican and whatever they could get on the trail.

Luke slid from his horse, stretching his legs, and apparently searching the countryside for any hint that someone followed. He finally unrolled a blanket on the ground, inviting her to sit.

She hesitated, not sure she wanted to have a sit-down meal with him.

But he disappeared into the bushes.

She enjoyed the reprieve. Her backside already ached, but she dared not complain.

Luke returned after a while with a handful of berries. "How about a treat?"

"Thank you." She took the dark fruit from him, devouring their sweetness.

He laughed. "Did it enter your mind to share?"

Pink colored her cheeks. "I'm sorry. I just thought you'd already—"

"I did. I just wanted to tease you."

A grin broke out. It was good to see a more playful side to him even if she was the object of his joke. They had several weeks to spend together. She guessed he intended to treat her with a bit of kindness along the way instead of his former indifference.

"I saw a rock schoolhouse when I rode through Justice City. Was that where you taught?"

She pushed up from the blanket, dusting off her dress. Sorrow surrounded her, its grip squeezing her heart. "Yes. Don't know if I'll ever be allowed to teach again even if I clear my name."

"Why not?" he asked. "You're innocent."

"Yes, but people will always wonder..."

"You can't help what people think. You know the truth. That should be good enough."

But it wasn't. She wanted her name cleared and her reputation returned.

Talking about the loss of her profession, whether temporary or permanent, grieved her heart. She wanted the conversation to end. "Maybe we should go?"

"We'll ride a few more hours and then rest the horses again, but I don't want to stop for the night until dusk. We've got to stay far enough ahead that no one can catch us."

She liked his plan. Even though it had been a while since there'd been any sign of Caldwell or his men, Luke had poked a hornet's nest when he went probing around Justice City. They were as good as dead if either the sheriff or her former boss caught up with them.

Luke didn't seem particularly worried. Maybe it was the life he lived that made him more composed. But the thought of dying by gunshot or hanging from a tree did not appeal. Her fear wasn't something she could easily hide.

"When Caldwell's men came by the cabin," she began. "Abigail told them I'd gone to Mexico."

"She's smart like that. Let's hope and pray that Caldwell isn't smarter."

But Caldwell hadn't stayed alive as long as he had because of stupidity. He'd stolen money from miners, framed her, murdered Malcolm, and all without leaving behind any proof. Then he'd filed a claim with the insurance company to have the miner's money restored—money he'd stolen in the first place. Criminally brilliant.

Of course, people had suspicions, but no one who wanted to remain alive dared to voice them. His ruthlessness preceded him. She was the only proof that slipped through his fingers, and Caldwell intended to do everything in his power to get rid of her, and now Luke.

"He won't stop until he knows I'm dead."

"We'll see about that," Luke said with confidence.

His words stirred a hope she prayed was not in vain.

12

As darkness drew near, Luke guided the horses up into the hillside and away from the canyons. He seemed to know a lot about the terrain. He moved with a resilient purpose, weaving about boulders and trees before stopping at a semi-hidden cave. "Let me go in first. I need to check for bears."

Her hand rose to still the lurching of her heart. "And if you find one?"

"We'll ride like the wind." He stopped at the entrance, showing her several deep marks on the rocks surrounding the cave. "See that? Bear claws. They like to sharpen them on the rocks."

A lump slid down Billie's throat. Was he teasing her again? A clammy sensation spread across her limbs. He disappeared inside. She listened for the slightest sound. It seemed like forever before he reappeared, wearing a smile, and holding up a dead rabbit. "Good news. No bears, and better news—I found supper."

By the time they finished dinner and tossed the remains down the hillside, stars lit the sky like specks of gold dust on a bed of ebony rocks. A faint breeze sifted about, moving in and out of the cave in a gentle swish.

Billie turned her face into the wind, enjoying the coolness. The scent of trees and damp earth wafted under her nose. "I can almost smell autumn. Guess I'll spend winter in Arkansas this year." The words made her melancholy.

A coyote sounded in the distance, and Luke tilted his head in curiosity. He gave a coyote call back as if expecting a response, but no sound came.

"How'd you learn to do that so well?"

"Comanche. My father's people."

She sat on the blanket only feet from him, her legs curled underneath her. He sat with knees bent and ankles crossed, much like she imagined his Comanche family and ancestors had sat. A fading campfire burned between them. There was something unsettling about being alone with him, but nothing she wanted to wish away.

"How did your father and mother come to marry?" Perhaps her question was too personal.

He didn't seem to mind. There was no hesitation or frown. His expression remained relaxed and open. "My mother's parents were missionaries and served the Comanche people. It was there where my mother and father met, fell in love, and got married. Her father performed the ceremony. When they all returned to Texas to start a sheep business, her father hoped his new son-in-law would learn the trade. But—" His gaze shifted away from hers. "My father went back to the old ways. He left my mother, married several other native women, came back to her long enough for

Abigail to be born and left again. He was happy Abigail looked like my mother—said her life would be easier that way."

"He didn't stay even though he had two children with your mother?"

"No. He never stayed anywhere." He reached down and stirred the fire with a twig. "He couldn't adjust to my mother's life nor did he want her with him and the Comanche. He said he wanted his children to learn the new ways. He believed the Comanche way was dying."

She waited for him to continue.

"My mother taught me to read and write. My grandfather taught Abigail and me to shoot. Besides the fact I looked so different than the rest of my family, it was a good life. My mother made sure of it." He grinned, laughing at a memory. "A traveling salesman brought his wares to our doorstep one time and commended my mother for taking in a savage. Said he admired her act of Christian charity. But my mother got so angry she chased him off the front porch with a wooden spoon. He never came back."

The sound of the dying fire crackled and sputtered pieces of hot ash.

She let the moment hang between them before asking, "When was the last time you saw your father?"

"When I was in my teens," he said. "He came and got me. Said I had to become a man to be recognized as a Comanche. Go through a rite of passage." His voice grew sullen, and his stare darkened. "I learned many things from his people, and I did what he said, but I never felt at home with the tribe, and I never finished the rite. My mother was against the ceremony, and so was my grandfather. I had become a white man on the inside even though I looked like my father on the outside."

"You say that like it's a bad thing."

"To him, it was a great disappointment. So, he returned me to my mother, and that was the last time I saw him."

Pain froze within his features. The rejection must have rent his young soul. How could a father be so cruel? Did he not realize that his son and daughter needed him — that his wife needed him?

"So now you know the whole story of my life."

She doubted that.

"We should get some sleep." He rose, taking their horse's reins and leading them deeper into the cave.

Billie stood. "What can I do to help out?"

He stopped, looking at her as if she'd grown a horn. "Just close your eyes and enjoy the rest."

"Right here?"

"Yes. On the blanket. I'll cover you up."

"Where will you sleep?"

"Outside the cave, so I can hear if anyone or anything comes."

He walked toward his saddle, removing the blanket.

Billie locked her hands together, prim and proper. "Luke, I don't know what to say except thank you. I didn't know if I'd make it to Arkansas by myself."

"You'd make it. Any woman who can point a gun

at a bounty hunter and tell him to drop his holster without blinking—"

"Just so you know—" She tried to hide the grin. "I was scared out of my wits. It wasn't bravery that made me do it. It was fear—fear of dying in the dirt and no one knowing what happened to me."

He took a step toward her. "You won't have to worry about that ever again."

Her breath came faster.

His gaze lowered to her lips.

Every part of her said yes, but she stepped back and the moment splintered. Something had happened—a spark, a flame, or maybe a full-fledged fire had ignited, and the thought terrified her even as it thrilled her.

"Good night, Billie Jo." He held out the blanket.

She blinked several times to regroup. Her throat tightened. "Good night, Luke." Her voice was a bare whisper. She took the blanket with trembling fingers and dampness clinging to her lashes that should not have been there. The man did something to her that no man had ever done. He stirred her.

With a glance, he made her knees weak. With a whisper, he siphoned desire from her being. Her lips longed to taste his—to search past their sweetness into the fullness of his mouth. She had never had such thoughts. How dare her flesh betray her. Didn't she have enough on her mind?

Luke Lancaster would get her to Arkansas and then leave. Was that the man she wanted to give her heart and soul? No. She had not waited this long just to choose a vagabond as the love of her life. She did not want a relationship like Luke's mother and father. She wanted something solid—something that would last.

Like an apple tree among the trees of the woods, so is my beloved among the sons. I sat down in the shade with great delight, and his fruit was sweet to my taste. Words she did not want to recall flooded her mind, leaping off the pages of the Bible that still lay beside her bed in Justice City. *Beloved? He is not my beloved! He is a bounty hunter with a wanderlust spirit. How else can he know the paths, waters, and caves so well?*

Let this trip end soon, Father. I can't bear to remain in the man's presence. My heart is weak. I fear it has betrayed me.

~*~

Luke stared out at the sky, chastising himself. He'd wanted to kiss her. She knew it. He knew it. Probably the skunks, squirrels, spiders, and snakes knew it. That would've been stupid. Three weeks on the road with a woman he'd come to have feelings for—and when had that happened anyway? Had it occurred when he learned she'd taken care of Abigail and little Henry in their time of need? When he heard Molly's version of what happened at the bank? Or had it been when he saw her in that blue dress—looking soft and inviting? Maybe it was all three and then some. Maybe it happened when he first saw her at the river's edge and realized there was more than met the eye.

He'd lived his life purposely not getting too attached to any woman. His line of work wasn't conducive to a wife and family. So why'd he let his mind go there with Billie?

Thoughts pushed against reason—thoughts he tried to shove away as fast as they came. He could never be with Billie. He could never be with any woman—not as long as he worked for the agency. Yet, the notion continued to gnaw at him as if sent from a divine Source that would not be silenced.

He peered into the cave. Through the moon's rays, he could see the curve of her back, and her hair splayed out past her shoulders, down to her waist, and onto the blanket. How had a teacher from the small town of Justice City, Texas, got in such trouble? Was it as simple as being at the wrong place at the wrong time, or was it more than that? Perhaps a setup from the very beginning?

It was impossible to conceive Billie Jo ever deserving what was happening to her right now. He had to get back and talk to Theo. Surely, the agency had their undercover deputy in place by now. And couldn't they look at past records and see the total amount deposited in Caldwell's bank and the total amount moved out?

Caldwell and McGregor would end up in jail or dangling from a noose. They had to pay for what they'd done. People didn't commit such crimes and get away with them. He'd see to it. But until then, he had to keep Billie Jo alive. She was the only one who could tell the truth.

It wasn't time to let her know that someone followed him. As long as the tracker kept his distance, no need to add more worry to her shoulders. She already carried enough. Besides, what could she do about it besides look over her shoulder every few seconds? Then whoever it was would grow suspicious and up their game. Better their stalker remain unaware. Luke would deal with it soon enough.

A low rumbling sound raked through the bushes only feet in front of him—moving upward toward the cave. A loud huff sounded and then the snapping of branches. An animal odor wafted that curled his toes.

Luke jumped up, climbing into a tree to get a better look. He shimmied up the bark, glancing out into the illuminated night.

Please let it be a wild boar or a deer or anything but a—

A massive black bear lifted his nose into the air.

No!

At least the beast would find the rabbit remains from their dinner first. That would give him time to wake Billie, grab the horses, and get out of there. When it came to short sprints a black bear could take a horse every time. Their only hope was a strong head start. He just had to remain quiet enough and pray that the wind wouldn't shift before he made his move.

With teeth clenched and muscles wound taut, Luke maneuvered silently down the tree with clean movements that landed him on the ground a good twenty feet away from the bear. A hungry bear could cross that space before he had time to run. He moved with quick precision toward the cave, walking as the

Comanche had shown him to keep from making a sound.

Billie slept soundly.

He shook her shoulder.

She rose up onto an elbow and stared at him in startled confusion.

He held his fingers to his lips. "Don't make a sound. We've got company."

"Caldwell?"

"No. A bear. Grab the blanket. Get on your horse. We've got to move. Now."

She stood without a word. Her horse neighed as she pulled herself up.

A groan slipped from Luke's lips. "Go now!" he yelled.

Billie nudged her horse, and they flew out the cave opening, Luke directly behind her just as the bear broke through the brush. Wild eyes shone green in the light of the full moon as a shadow rose and growled, showing teeth that still held blood and bone fragments from the rabbit carcass.

Her horse rushed forward, sensing danger was near, Billie Jo holding tight to the reins. She glanced back once, her loosed hair whipping about her face.

The bear moved toward them several feet, and Luke feared it would give chase, but it stopped and stood again—leaving them with a growl that felt as if it shook the entire hillside.

Luke didn't stop until they'd crossed a stream and then passed back over the water several miles down the dusty path. That would get rid of their scent.

Finally, he tugged on his reins, halting his horse on the bank, and letting him draw a heavy drink. "I know another place we can bed down for the night, but it's a few hours down the road."

Billie looked as if she might lose her dinner. Her hand rested on her belly. "I don't think I can sleep in another cave—not after seeing that bear so close."

"This isn't a cave. It's a house. One I've stayed at before while tracking outlaws."

Her hair cascaded down her shoulders and body in a shimmery, red-gold veil. He looked away, half afraid he might reach out and touch the silken threads. Now was not a good time to think such thoughts. She might laugh in his face, and he wouldn't blame her one bit. What would a beautiful teacher want with a half-breed bounty hunter? Even as the thought left his mind, another thought penetrated his soul. A powerful whisper—unexpected but piercing.

You are exactly who I created you to be. Exactly.

The thought shocked him so much that he held his breath for several seconds before finally exhaling. OK. He was who he was supposed to be. There was no questioning that truth. Now, he just wanted to understand what to do with the guilt of the past. Was that meant for his shoulders, too? Or was there a safe place to hide the pain where he'd never see it again? Did the same Voice Who'd spoken to him want him to suffer the burden of what had happened for the rest of his life?

There were no easy answers and certainly no profound response from the One he'd once called

Lord. Only the silence he'd come to expect any time he pressed into the pain.

13

Billie stood outside of Luke's aunt's home.

"You're welcomed here anytime." The attractive older woman ran her hand familiarly down Luke's shoulder. One gray brow lifted, and a dimple appeared in her chin. "And your pretty friend, too."

"Billie, this is my aunt."

Still pink-cheeked, Billie extended her hand. "Nice to meet you."

"You may call me Louise."

"Louise runs a stagecoach stop," Luke explained. "She almost always has a spare bed or two for a driver and passengers."

Morning light had begun to shine through the windows, but Billie was exhausted.

"We just need a few hours of rest. Then we'll be on our way." Luke told his aunt.

"On our way to where?" Louise asked, welcoming them both inside.

Buttered cornbread sat on the oven. Bacon lay across a skillet.

The delicious smell permeated the air, causing Billie's insides to churn. "Arkansas," she answered. "To stay with my family."

"Well, before your naps, why not enjoy a quick bite to eat? I just whipped up some breakfast. I'm expecting several visitors today, but there's plenty to go around."

Later, with a full belly and a comfortable mattress, Billie slept for several hours. She awakened at the tap on the door and Luke's voice from the other side.

"Time to ride."

She groaned and sat up, legs dangling over the side of the bed. It would be three weeks before they arrived at her Arkansas destination. It could not come soon enough. With a deep stretch, Billie reached her arms over her head then dropped them in her lap. She straightened the collar on her dress and smoothed out the wrinkles from the hard sleep.

"Now take some cornbread and bacon with you," Louise said as she gave Luke a hard squeeze. "It'll be a good supper later in the evening. And you remember what your momma always said. Look twice, for the night has a thousand eyes."

He chuckled. "That's what my father always said, not my mother."

"Oh, well, I knew it was one of them. But your momma always said to say your prayers, that I'm sure of."

"I can't remember the last time I prayed. Guess it was before—"

"That's not your fault, Luke." Her voice turned stern though love still lingered in her gaze. "Think how it'd make your momma feel, knowing you were blaming yourself or worse, blaming God for what happened. No one could know the girl was sick in the head. No one."

"The Comanche knew," he said, his words laced with bitterness. "That's why they sent her away."

"They've always had their ways. Our people lock them up in a sanitarium and throw away the key. The Comanches send them outside the village to make it on their own or die. Which way is better and which way is worse? I can't say. I only know that your momma is with the Lord, and she'd take a switch to your legs if she knew you hadn't talked to Him."

A fleeting expression flickered on Luke's face. "I know. I'm getting straight. But I need a little time, and God has seen fit to give it to me."

Billie's heart soothed in a way she could not explain. If only God could remove the guilt from her heart.

Malcolm was a good man. A believer. A widower who'd suffered so much, and then to die because of her. It was almost unbearable to ponder.

"I'll make the trip over the river real soon and meet Henry, Jr.," Louise said, taking the conversation a new direction. "Does he need anything?"

"A good blanket before winter arrives would be appreciated, I'm sure."

"A good blanket it'll be." She turned toward Billie. "Thank you for coming to visit. Maybe next time you can stay a while longer."

There'd never be a next time. But Billie smiled and let the older woman give her a quick hug before looking at Luke.

He led Billie toward a nearby barn where he guided their horses out into the fresh air. Both appeared refreshed, frisky, and ready to go.

A twinge of longing filled Billie's heart as she glanced back at the small house. Would she sleep in another bed before Arkansas? Funny the things she'd taken for granted. Cold water from a deep well. A soft down mattress for weary limbs. And an outhouse. Those were things she missed the most right now.

It was three hours later before they stopped for a rest, letting their horses sip from a clear, running stream.

Billie wasn't sure if they'd ventured into Arkansas yet, but the relentless heat had let up. Trees were taller and more plentiful.

Luke leaned on a boulder; one leg propped against the surface while the other remained on the ground. "Do you want me to get out the blanket so you can sit and stretch out a while?"

"No need for that. I've had plenty of sitting time."

"So now that we've spent a couple of days together and you know I'm not out for the bounty, why don't you tell me your version of what happened in the bank that day?"

She grimaced, looking away.

The horses continued to drink from the dancing stream, neither lifting their head. Several birds chirped and complained about the intrusion into their secluded forest area.

"So, why exactly are you helping me, Luke? If it's not for money, then why?"

He shrugged. "Do I need a reason?"

"People usually do have a reason for risking their life."

"Then, I guess I'm helping you because it's the right thing to do. I believe you're innocent."

"And that's it? That's the only reason?"

His expression held steady. "For now."

His response wasn't satisfactory, but she stayed quiet. For now.

"I've answered, so you owe me the same honesty. What happened at the bank? What part are you not telling?"

She swallowed hard, looking past him and the horses, gazing downstream.

His voice broke the silence binding them together as his strong arms crossed his broad chest. "All right, then. I'll tell you what I know from Molly. You worked for Caldwell part-time helping your friend Malcolm at the Justice City Bank."

The horses' slurping pushed water from one side of the bank to the other.

Her heart beat faster. "Malcolm figured out that Caldwell was dipping into the miner's gold. So, he wanted me to verify what he found out. Then, once we were both sure, Malcolm called Sheriff McGregor. Only McGregor didn't show up alone. He showed up with Clovis Caldwell, and McGregor shot Malcolm." She paused, letting her words hang in the air before finishing. "I barely escaped with my life." She lifted her gaze toward him. The heat from barely contained tears burned her eyes.

He leaned against the boulder as if he had all afternoon to enjoy a leisurely rest.

"I left out one important detail." Her voice sounded flat, even to her own ears. "Malcolm didn't want to go to McGregor. He wanted to go to the Texas Rangers since the gold was coming in from out of state—said he trusted them to get the proper authorities involved."

"That would've been smart," Luke said. "Why didn't he?"

"Because of me," she said. "I told him to tell McGregor first. I'm the one who brought the sheriff and Clovis to the bank."

~*~

Luke stared at her, his mind returning to Molly's words in the store. Billie Jo wouldn't purposely hurt anyone.

"It's my fault Malcolm is dead. If I'd just let him do what he thought was best—" Her voice broke and her chin quivered. "I thought I was so smart. Thought I was doing the right thing. If only I'd—"

Luke pulled her into his arms. She buried her face in his chest as the tears flooded her eyes, poured over her cheeks, and dampened his shirt. Her shoulders shook, and limbs grew weak against him.

He held on as her knees folded, keeping her close and secure within a strong embrace. Minutes and countless tears passed before either said a word.

"Billie Jo, listen to me," he began, his voice a

whisper against her ear. "I know what it's like to carry that burden. It's not your fault McGregor is a dishonest sheriff, or Caldwell is a thief." *It's not your fault that girl was insane.* He ignored the voice in his head. "You know Malcolm would never want you to blame yourself." *Just as your mother would never want you to blame yourself.*

Luke grimaced. How easy it was to toss out words when someone was hurting or needed answers. Advice never sounded quite as good when it boomeranged back and hit one square between the eyes.

In a sense, they were the same. Both felt responsible for another person's death—a person they'd genuinely loved. There was no turning back the clock. There was no making a wrong suddenly right. Justice and revenge would not bring back loved ones. Only God could heal their guilt and soothe the pain of their regret. Only God could carry the burden of their past. Even still, they had a part to play in the process. They had to release their hold, and that was easier said than done.

"I'm not sure why I was keeping all that inside. As if I had to carry my pain as punishment for what I'd done. But I know that's not God's will. He is loving and kind and overflowing with mercy and forgiveness."

He nodded, suddenly unable to speak. She was right, but he didn't want to hear it. Not yet.

"Abigail told me about the woman who set fire to your mother's home. We share similar scars, Luke. Maybe that's why God brought us together."

Pain sliced his heart. He wished she'd quit talking.

"Is the woman who set fire to your momma's house still in the woods?"

"I don't know. But I wonder what I'd do if I ever saw her again."

"What would your mother want you to do?"

"Something impossible."

Billie Jo leaned back to look at his face. She did not find an answer.

"She'd want me to forgive her. And myself."

14

The next two weeks held unexpected joy at unexpected times.

Luke watched her on occasion as if he had something on his mind. But he never put the thoughts into words. Was his affection toward her growing as rapid as hers toward him? It certainly seemed that way, but was that the truth or the wishes of an appreciative woman?

Luke was masculine and handsome. The few times they entered a town, women would take a second glance. But it was his spirit that captivated her heart.

There was kindness in the way he always accommodated her needs and in the care he gave the horses. Even the occasions when he had to kill for them to eat, he did so swiftly and treated the gift of nourishment with respect—thanking God for it. And he'd begun to pray.

Most were brief sentences thanking God. For the sunset. For another morning of life. For a soft place to rest their head. And, for no bears. She realized that Luke delighted in the simple things in life, and she found herself deeply moved at that part of his being.

He talked about his father some, but most of the

memories he shared with her were of his sister, mother, and grandparents. They were a close family, much like her own—minus a steadfast father.

She dreaded saying good-bye. They'd shared a closeness and camaraderie on the trail that would not have come from months of courting. He knew she groaned in her sleep, and she knew he never slept soundly. If she even rolled over, his head would turn her direction.

He'd talked more about his family and the love he had for the natives and the settlers. He even talked about his job and how he almost had enough money saved to buy a small ranch and start building a herd. He had hopes and dreams and didn't mind sharing them.

She shared hers, too. Her heart ached to return to teaching. She loved what she did and felt honored to have such a profession. "I'd do it for free if I had to, but it's in my blood to teach."

They'd started praying for one another—for the desires of their hearts to be met and for the Lord to keep them safe. They prayed for wisdom and discernment, and they prayed for a heart that was quick to forgive and let go of the guilt that was never theirs to carry.

They were in Arkansas now, she was sure. Less than a week away from her destination. While her excitement soared at seeing her family and finally being able to stop looking over her shoulder, her heart shredded at the thought of leaving Luke.

The sun had started to descend when Luke

pointed upward toward a cliff. A rocky ledge capped the top, providing shelter. "Let's camp up there tonight. Even if the weather turns bad, we'll be protected."

The path was steeper than any other they'd used. "Is it safe to travel up that grade on horseback?"

"We'll leave the horses here," he said. "They won't venture far and can find shelter in the trees if it starts to rain."

She'd gotten so used to sleeping outside, that the sounds of crickets and frogs no longer bothered her. She welcomed their song, knowing it meant that predators were not around. It was when the sounds stopped that she grew tense.

Thankfully, that had only happened a couple of times, and Luke had to run off a fox and a rogue coyote. Otherwise, the nights had become peaceful, and the canopy of stars more beautiful every time she looked upward and said her prayers.

Luke never seemed as relaxed as she, but she figured that was just because of what he did for a living. A bounty hunter was always on edge—always on the hunt, and always looking out for whoever else might be out to do the same.

The more ruthless bounty hunters were known to kill other bounty hunters to get the reward money. She knew that wasn't Luke, but that didn't mean someone else wasn't on their tail, looking for the perfect opportunity to rid him of his captive.

~*~

Luke opened his eyes, hearing the muted movement of heavy feet. He slid down from the tree where he'd made his bed for the night amongst the thick red maple bows. The sound came again. Whoever it was didn't intend on remaining unseen. He stopped in his tracks, speaking into the faint breeze. "Show yourself."

The sound evaporated. He glanced over where Billie had fallen asleep. His heart slammed into his chest. She was gone. He took off running toward where he'd last seen her.

"Billie!"

She screamed just before a hard thud hit him on his right shoulder, knocking him off balance and twisting him sideways. He scrambled to regain his footing, still moving forward. Another thud hit him, this time on the back of the head. Luke's feet slipped out from underneath him. A flash of light shook his vision just as darkness came with the heaviness of a hammer.

When he awoke, daylight surrounded him. The back of his head throbbed, and his shoulder ached. His boots and shirt were missing. All he wore were his trousers and incessant pain.

Where am I? His memory returned with a flood of questions. *Where's Billie?* He was lying face down on a wool blanket. He rolled over, staring up into the top of a teepee. Luke tried to rise.

A low, rumbling voice came from nearby. "Lay back down."

Luke snapped his head sideways then groaned in

agony at the sudden movement. It was Mighty Bow, the war chief, and the last person he wanted to see. He held onto his composure, knowing he could not lose it now, or he'd be as good as dead. "Where's Billie?"

"You prefer the white woman over my daughter?"

The man was the most respected council leader in the tribe. He had a six-inch scar down one side of his cheek from a fight he won and another eight-inch scar down his right arm from a fight he'd lost. His hooded eyes held nothing but contempt.

Luke had to be careful how he answered. "I am taking Billie to her family. She is not my woman."

A low growl rolled across thin lips.

"Where is she?" Luke repeated, trying to keep his voice at a respectful level.

"Safe." Mighty Bow stood up and walked out the teepee flap.

Luke tried to rise but lay back down. Nausea rushed to the back of his throat. The man had given him a concussion and maybe knocked his shoulder out of joint. He'd used an old trick. Got him to react without thinking when he saw Billie gone.

Where was Billie anyway? Probably scared out of her wits. He needed to find her—to make sure she was all right and to explain to his tribesmen what was happening. Before he had a chance to think another thought, White Feather entered the teepee.

Though a good ten years younger than him, she was a beautiful woman who could marry any man in the tribe. Why she'd set her heart on him, he didn't understand. Probably because she knew he was the last person her father wanted her to marry.

"I brought you soup," she said. "It has medicine. For your head."

"What are you doing here?"

"You would not return to marry me. So, my father brought us together. The celebration will take place tomorrow." She kneeled beside him then held out a spoon filled with steaming liquid. "Eat."

He did as she said, thinking of a thousand ways to escape but knowing he would have to get Billie out with him. Then what? Could they make it to Arkansas without getting an arrow in the heart? He wasn't sure, but one thing he did know—he was far more worried about the natives than Caldwell's men. At least with Caldwell's posse, he had a chance.

Luke pushed the spoon away after several slurps. "How long have you followed us?"

"Weeks," she said.

"White Feather, isn't there someone else you'd rather marry? I'm much older, and I don't know how to live the native way. I was raised by my mother, remember?"

"To the shame of your father."

He gritted his teeth, more from her words than the pain that still held him captive. "You don't have to remind me of that."

"I choose you," she said, lifting her chin in a serene pose that spoke of her finality. "You will not change my mind. I will teach you the native ways. Even old mules can learn new paths."

He thought about being offended but shrugged it

off. "I'm not trying to change your mind. I'm trying to make you think about what you're doing and why you're doing it. If you're wanting to annoy your father, there are other ways—not nearly so permanent."

"Are you done with your soup?"

"Yes and thank you. It was good."

She stood up to go.

Luke's opportunity was slipping by. "Is Billie OK?"

"Yes. She is protected." She stood at the entry, the half-empty soup bowl in her hand. "Why is it you do not desire me? Am I not pretty enough?"

"You're beautiful," he said. "You know that."

"Then what is it?" Her voice turned stern.

"We're from different worlds. I wouldn't be happy in yours, and you wouldn't be happy in mine."

Defiance darkened her eyes. "How do you know I wouldn't be happy in yours?"

"I just know."

"It doesn't matter what you know. Tomorrow, we will marry. My father will see to it."

"White Feather, you don't want to do this. Trust me."

"You trust me," she said. "It is already done." White Feather dropped the teepee flap and walked out

Luke groaned and began to pray.

Billie was most likely praying, too.

15

Luke fought against falling asleep, but the medicine would not let him stay awake. Before he closed his eyes, he prayed for God to heal him and make a way out of the situation he faced. Tomorrow, White Feather expected him to marry her. Her father, the war chief, intended to make sure it happened—even though it was obvious he despised the thought.

As the early afternoon light shone through the teepee, his strength returned. He rose, sitting up straight to give his head a chance to stop spinning. An idea came to him during the night—an idea that might save Billie's life, even if it cost him his own.

He reached inside the lining of his trousers where he always kept a knife carefully sewed into the fabric. He tugged on the tacking and slid the sharp blade from its hiding place. With a determined bent to his brow, he made his way to the teepee entry. He peeled back the flap. Just as he suspected, a couple of young braves stood watch.

Both jumped when they saw him standing at the entrance.

"Go get Mighty Bow," Luke ordered. "I need to have a word with him."

One disappeared while the other stared, mouth slightly agape. Luke glanced around. There were no more than twelve teepees. It looked like only the council had come to witness the wedding. The rest of the tribe must have stayed behind, waiting for their return.

The young warrior pulled himself together, speaking in rough English. "Be good to her, or I will kill you myself."

"Good to whom?" Luke asked.

"White Feather."

"So, you are in love with her, too. Like half the men in the tribe."

"Only a fool would not be," he stammered in indignation. "She can shoot an arrow like a falcon can catch a rat. And she is beautiful like a flower. More beautiful than anyone I have ever seen. Her children will be chiefs. What man would not be honored to have White Feather at his side?"

Luke walked back inside, sat down and waited for Mighty Bow to appear. When the great chief walked into the teepee, he rose out of respect. "Thank you for coming."

Mighty Bow grunted and sat.

Luke sat opposite him. "I know you do not want me to marry your daughter. I'm not sure why she wants to marry me. And as beautiful as she is—the most beautiful woman in the entire tribe—I do not wish to marry her. I would not want to live with the Comanche."

"What you want does not matter. You will do as

my daughter wishes."

"Yes," Luke said. "I will. But only after I see Billie on her horse and riding away with no one following after her."

He snorted. "You think you can barter? Like guns for whiskey? My daughter for your woman?"

"I've already said," Luke began. "Billie is not my woman."

"I do not agree to your terms."

Luke showed him the knife. "I will cut the vein on my neck and bleed to death right here in this teepee." He did not flinch. "You know I will do it."

"I would stop you," the proud warrior stated with certainty.

"You might. But your daughter would be disgraced."

Mighty Bow frowned. "We do not want the white woman. She would only bring trouble. She can leave."

"But first I want to see her and make sure she is well."

"You do not trust me?"

Luke shook his head in disbelief. "You about knocked my head off and kidnapped us both. I want to see her for myself. That's not too much to ask."

"Very well." Mighty Bow stood at the teepee entrance. "Bring me the white woman." He turned back around, motioning for Luke to stand. "Come outside. There is more for you to see."

With the knife firmly in his grasp, he stepped out into the center of the teepees. They formed a full circle with a small fire in the middle.

From Luke's peripheral vision, he saw the young warrior bringing Billie toward him. Her hands were tied behind her back. Strands of copper hair fell about her shoulders, but other than that, she looked unharmed.

"Luke..." Tears filled her eyes but did not fall.

Several braves and a few older tribesmen stepped out of their tents. White Feather appeared, standing beside her mother and a younger sister.

Mighty Bow stood several inches taller than all the other men. His booming voice commanded attention, and his overpowering presence demanded respect. "Our brother has asked that we let his woman go free."

"She is not my woman," Luke said.

"Then, you don't mind if we give her to another?" Mighty Bow teased.

"She's not yours to give. She is her own."

"After she is gone, we will celebrate," Mighty Bow stated. "Luke and White Feather will marry."

White Feather lifted her chin, though her eyes remained on her father.

A native man stepped from the woods, drawing everyone's attention. The man stood tall and regal, just as large as Mighty Bow but with a familiar look to his eyes that caused Luke's mind to spin out of control. How was it possible? He had not seen his father in more than a decade. Yet here he stood, looking older but somehow the same.

"My son will not marry your daughter," he said.

Billie's eyes widened, and she turned toward Luke.

He offered a comforting bob of his head, though he wasn't sure what was about to happen.

"You do not usually participate in the council," Mighty Bow said. "You are a lone wolf who comes and goes as he pleases. You have no right to speak."

"I have every right." The man stepped near. "My son is not bound to marry your daughter. He is free to marry whom he wills."

"As much as I would like my daughter to choose another," Mighty Bow continued, though more subdued. "She has chosen. She will marry your son."

"But my son has not chosen her. This marriage will not be."

Luke felt the hairs on the back on his neck rise. The situation was escalating. That was never a good sign. He appreciated his long, lost father coming to his defense, but Mighty Bow was right. His father was a lone wolf. Why he chose to appear now, Luke wasn't sure. Was he an answer to prayer or the evidence of his impending death?

"My father swore I could marry any native I chose," White Feather stated, her voice cracking through the air like the sting of a whip. "I choose your son."

"Yes," Luke's father said. "Mighty Bow did make such a promise. I was there when he said those words. But Luke is not a native. He never finished the rite of passage. He is not a true Comanche. He is a white man. You *will* choose another."

Mighty Bow looked to Luke. "Is this true?"

Luke paused. His answer mattered. "It is true."

The war chief almost smiled but refrained. "Then, he is right." He looked to his daughter. "You are free to marry any native you choose. Luke is not a native. He is born of the white woman and woven into the white woman's ways. He is not Comanche."

Her eyes narrowed, turning upon Luke's father. "This is your fault. Why did you come back now?"

"Because my son needs me."

"Then if we will not marry," White Feather began, hatred seething from her tone and the hardness of her glare. "We kill his woman. What is she to us?"

Billie's jaw dropped, but she struggled to regain her composure. The hands of the warriors tightened on her arms. "I have done nothing to you. Why would you—"

"Let the white woman go," his father said. "She is already wanted for murder in the white world."

Luke frowned but remained silent. How could his father possibly know that fact?

"The white man will kill her. Why should we? This is not the time to go to war. She is not worth the blood of our braves." Luke's father stood firm.

Mighty Bow looked to the young warriors holding Billie's arms. "Set her free."

White Feather's brows pinched together in anger as she struck Luke with a pointed stare. "I will call down the spirits of our ancestors upon you. You look Comanche, but your heart is turned from your people. They will destroy you! You do not belong in our world or any other world."

Luke figured she was wrong. God had made him

exactly as he should be. He prayed for the tribe, but his trust rested upon his faith in God. With doubts settled and God's mercy tenderly applied to his heart, Luke was determined to hold onto his faith even harder than before.

"I will show you the way back to your path," his father said, speaking directly to Luke and ignoring Billie. "Then you are free to go where you choose." His gaze shifted to Mighty Bow. "If that is acceptable with the council."

Mighty Bow gave him a dismissive bob of his head. "Go."

White Feather turned and stomped away, leaving Luke wondering if he'd truly heard the last of her. She was not a woman used to being told "No". She was the war chief's daughter and war coursed through her blood in fiery, red rage.

Luke motioned for Billie.

The two braves released their hold and she walked toward him.

"Turn around." She did, without question. He removed her leather bonds with a firm yank. "You're free." Then he lifted his chin. "We're both free. Let's go."

16

"Did the natives harm you?" Luke asked, his gaze piercing as he examined her from head to foot for injuries.

A flush rose upon her cheeks at that pointed stare. "No. But one woman threatened to cut off my nose and another threatened to boil me and eat me alive."

Luke's father laughed aloud. "We do not eat people—especially white people. It would make us ill. Keep us running to the bushes."

Billie laughed, with relief. Despite the amusement she saw in Luke's eyes, she also sensed something else simmering beneath the surface—a dark brooding, like a distant storm drawing near to blue skies at a slow, but threatening pace.

Luke's father led the way. She didn't know his name yet and hesitated to ask. She knew many years had passed since the two had talked. What were they thinking now? She could not imagine the emotions surging about their hearts and minds, yet they remained stoic and silent.

They rode for almost an hour, no one speaking as the trail dipped, twisted, and finally came to a clearing. A stream rolled from the hillside, cutting a wide path of moving water. Tall trees stood off in the distance, dense but welcoming. A whitetail doe bounded off into the foliage, disappearing from sight.

Luke's father waited for him at a steep rise. He pointed to a high place just before the stream crossing. "See that path?"

"Yes. It's the place we were resting before I got knocked on the head." Silence hung between them for several seconds before Luke asked, almost accusatory. "Is this where you say good-bye?"

"Before we part ways. Let's fish."

"Fish?"

"Yes."

Luke glanced back over his shoulder, his gaze lingering upon Billie's features. "Looks as if we're fishing."

"Fishing sounds good," she said, not wanting to cause any disruption. Besides, she was hungry, and the thought of fish in her belly sounded quite pleasant.

In just a few minutes, Luke's father had speared five fish—enough for them to share.

Luke had sent her on a mission to find berries, and she'd come back with her hands full.

Over dinner, she learned his father's name was Walking Stick. He'd been thin in his younger years, and everyone teased him, but as he'd grown older, the name remained. He was still lean, but more muscular and with chiseled features, much like his son.

As they sat around the fire, Walking Stick finished the last of his fish and slumped forward, looking older than she'd noticed before. It was odd how his expression never changed. Whether he joked or gave instruction, his features remained somber. Only his eyes seemed to laugh or show sorrow—never his face.

The older man spoke, looking into the dying embers of the fire. "I was sorry to hear of your mother's death."

"You and I will get along better if you do not mention her," Luke said with a sudden iciness.

Billie's spine stiffened. Would they argue or fight?

Walking Stick did not speak for several seconds. "The woman who set her house on fire died in a fire of her own making."

Luke's chest rose then fell.

Billie wished the conversation would cease. She feared the storm would overtake them all.

"Now how can I forgive her?" Luke asked his father.

"I do not know," Walking Stick replied.

Billie rose. "I should leave you two alone." She looked back to where the horses nibbled grass near the tree line. "I'll check on the horses."

"Don't go," Luke said, almost as if it were an order.

Drawn to those dark eyes—penetrating and hard yet tender at the same time—Billie paused. Could any man stir more conflicting emotions within her soul? One minute she wanted to run from him, and the next, she wanted to run into his arms. Nothing made sense, except for an inner knowing that the two men needed this time alone. Walking Stick would soon depart, and their moment, perhaps their last, would vanish.

"You need this," she said to Luke. "More than you know."

She turned and hurried away before he had a chance to call her name again.

~*~

"She is a wise woman," Walking Stick said. "You would do well to have her by your side in life. She sees with her heart. Not just her eyes."

"I do not need courting advice from you," Luke snapped. After several more seconds of silence, he exhaled hard. "I don't know what to think. I haven't seen you in almost ten years. Then you show up to rescue me, and I'm supposed to be grateful."

"No one said you had to be grateful. I came because you are my son. I have watched you grow, Luke. You have not seen me, but I have seen you. I watched you learn to shoot. I watched how you took care of your mother. You've become the man I always wanted you to become."

Luke swallowed hard. There were so many words he wanted to say. He'd rehearsed this moment a hundred times. But now, his mind felt numb with confusion. The anger seemed grotesque in the face of this man who no longer looked larger than life. The very emotion that had sustained him now seemed to betray him.

Walking Stick turned toward him for the first time since they'd sat down, giving him his full attention. Wrinkles lined the edge of his eyes and lips. Gray hair wove throughout the magnificent black braids. "You may not have finished the Comanche rite of passage, but you've become more of a man than most I've met. I will name you Golden Warrior."

"Golden Warrior." Luke blinked in confusion. "Why?"

"You are mighty and strong, like your mother—the woman with the golden hair and a warrior's heart."

Luke rose. He wasn't sure what to say or if he should say anything. "My mother loved you. Why didn't you stay?"

"The war chief gave you that answer. I am a lone wolf who finds no rest with others. If I could have stayed anywhere, it would have been with your mother."

His answer annoyed Luke. "Don't just say words to make things all right between us. You abandoned me. You abandoned Abigail. But most importantly, you abandoned your wife."

Walking Stick rose slowly. "Do you think your life would have been better if I'd stayed?" He shook his head. "No, Luke. Your neighbors would have pushed you away—fearful of the savage who lived amongst them. We'd already seen it happen. It hurt your mother, and I could not bear to see her cry another tear because of me."

His words were truth. His mother had told him so. Still, that did not make the reality of rejection hurt any less. Even now, it felt like the tip of a barb—a painful reminder of all he'd missed.

"That is just an excuse not to live up to your

responsibilities," Luke said. "A way to make what you did sound honorable in your own ears. But speak the truth. It is just us here—father and son. You left because you could and because you wanted to leave. No other reason."

"I was young, and I thought I was doing what was best."

"Best for whom?"

Walking Stick looked away. "Perhaps I should go now."

"No," Luke said. "You came back, and now I deserve the chance to speak." The wind seemed to rise out of nowhere, a gentle breeze that sifted throughout the trees. "I needed you growing up. I always needed you, and you weren't there. Abigail needed you, and our mother needed you."

"The winter that lasted too long when your food storage was empty, I was the one who left fresh meat at your door. You thought it was someone from your church. When your sister became ill and almost died from food poisoning, I brought the remedy and left it on the step so your mother would find it. You thought it was a neighbor or even an angel. When your sister had the little girl who died, I was there. When Henry was born, I waited outside the house for days— listening to your sister's cries of pain and then her tears of joy. Do not say I was not there. I was there. Always in the shadows, but there."

"In the shadows?" Luke felt his chest crushed with the agony of years without a father—made worse by the realization he'd been so close, and yet so far. "I would have rather had your presence. All the neighbors could have hated us, but if I'd had you, that would not have mattered."

"You say that now, but—"

"I needed you. We all needed you."

Something moved in a nearby brush. Luke turned just as several birds fluttered their wings and flew into the sky. He squinted into the descending sun—its brightness blinding him from what lay on the other side. He turned back to Walking Stick.

The older man's eyes remained fixed on the brush. "Then I made a mistake," Walking Stick said. "Can you forgive me for that? Or will you spend your entire life hating me for something neither of us can change?"

An arrow whizzed past Luke's face, hitting his father square in the chest and knocking him to the ground with a muted thud.

Luke wailed, pulling his gun from its holster and falling to his knees at his father's side.

Walking Stick stared at him, alive but bleeding like a river bursting through a dam.

Luke stood up, rushing into the brush without thinking.

In the distance, White Feather jumped on a horse, digging her heels into its flesh before riding off bareback into the woods at a wild pace.

He slammed his gun into his holster then hurried back to his father's side.

Billie made it to them, her breath coming in heaving gasps and her face as pale as the dry stones that lined the edge of the creek bed. "I heard you scream and—" She stopped, her eyes opening wide at the sight of all the blood.

"We've got to save him. I need your help."

Walking Stick looked at his son and closed his eyes.

17

"What if she comes back?" Billie asked. "What if she tries to kill you next?"

"White Feather won't ever return," Luke said. "There are serious consequences for killing a member of the council. Her own father would hang her."

Billie's stomach revolted at the thought.

Luke lifted his father's head, offering him a drink of something from a smaller canteen that he took from his father's saddlebag. The smell was horrible. "This will help him rest. Heat my knife over the fire. I will have to remove the arrow." He withdrew a folded cloth from the same saddlebag.

"But he's lost so much blood. Let him regain his strength."

"The sooner he can begin healing the better."

Billie grimaced as Luke guided the arrow from his father's flesh, turning her head away to hide the tears of anguish. The point had pushed deep within Walking Stick's chest. With the arrow pulled out, blood flowed bright and new.

Luke remained tense and focused as he poured the strong liquid over part of the cloth, then gently guided it around the circumference of the wound, pressing it inside. His father moaned. Luke drew back. He then wrapped the cloth around his father's body, tying it in a hard knot at his side. Every inch of his fingers was stained red.

"We will see what it looks like in a few hours," Luke said. "If blood continues to soak through, we know that he will not live. I will go to the creek and wash my hands."

Billie got Walking Stick a blanket from his pack. She was glad to see he was not shivering. His breathing, though shallow, remained steady. Surely, that was a good sign.

"We will stay camped here for a while." Luke returned from the creek. "I'll keep a watch tonight for Caldwell's men. In the morning, I'll rest, and you can keep watch."

She was too exhausted to argue. Billie lay down only feet from Walking Stick, closing her eyes and welcoming slumber. The smell of coffee woke her during the wee morning hours. She rose onto her forearm.

Luke drew the cup to his lips. His gaze remained on his father—an older and taller but almost identical version of the son.

"How did he do through the night?"

Luke's gaze darted toward her. "He's alive. I wish Abigail could be here. She barely remembers him."

"When he gets better, maybe he'll go visit her. Now that he's reappeared in your life, it won't be so difficult to remain."

"Maybe," he said, but it was obvious he didn't

believe that would happen.

She pushed the covers away, rising to her feet. "I'll trade places with you so you can get some sleep."

He yawned. "I need to rest, but I also need to eat." He stood to his full height. "I'll be back soon." He strode from sight, entirely impressive in his strength and stature. His father may not have raised him, but he certainly left his imprint upon him in every aspect of his imposing presence.

After they ate, Luke curled up and fell asleep, leaving Billie alone with her thoughts. Her relatives in Arkansas were not far away. Only a few days' journey but leaving was impossible. She had to believe that God had not forgotten them. He knew what was going on, and any anxiety she felt for the delay was purely selfish.

She pictured Abigail enjoying time with her husband and baby Henry. Henry, Sr., would be home by now, and the thought brought her peace. If Caldwell's men showed up again, at least Abigail would have someone there with her. Then she thought of her parents and siblings. How worried they must be. As soon as it was safe, she would get word to them. And she thought of the children in her schoolroom. They would probably have a new teacher by now, though she hoped they still thought of her fondly. She certainly cared a great deal for them all. So many people, and all ripped away from her like a season suddenly ending.

It almost seemed impossible to recall the predictability of her world only a month ago compared to her life now. She longed for a bit of boredom and mundane routine. What she wouldn't give to scrub laundry, peel potatoes, and bake rolls for the Sunday dinner with family and friends. Would she ever see those days again or would she remain a criminal on the run for her entire life?

Walking Stick groaned, and she moved toward him.

Luke had heard him and was already at his side. "It's OK," Luke whispered. "You'll be OK."

The older man reached out his hand and touched Luke's arm. Then his face twisted in a wince, and he drew his hand toward his chest. Luke checked the bandages, finding blood had seeped through.

"We've got to change his dressing."

"I can do it," Billie said, her heart overflowing with compassion. "You need to rest."

"I can't rest. Not now. I want to help."

She started to argue then thought better of it. This could be his last night with his father. She did not want to interfere or take that away. *Father God, let this man live. They've wasted so many years. Give them a chance to know one another—to love one another.*

When the sun rose, Luke caught some more fish and cooked it over the fire.

They sat in the cool shade, occasionally talking, but mostly silent as Walking Stick slept.

Luke leaned back against a large boulder as he kept watch over his father.

Billie wandered toward the stream, determined to bathe in its cool waters. She found a secluded spot away from view of the campsite and removed her dress and pantaloons. She dipped her clothes in the water several times, washing away the dust then laying them across a rock to dry in the warm sun's rays. She rinsed her hair and cleansed away the grime. She scrubbed her scalp then used the mud from the stream to polish her skin. It felt good to bathe in the stream waters. She wiggled her toes when minnows came near, scaring them away. Only when she felt completely refreshed and clean did she rise out of the waters and put on her sun-dried clothes. She twisted her hair into a braid then tucked it atop her head.

Luke greeted her with a smile when she returned, standing just outside the campsite. "Feel better?"

"Much."

"I think I'll do the same." He reached up and began to unbutton his shirt.

"Can you not wait until you're at the water to undress?" she huffed, shocked at his casual attitude.

"Why so embarrassed? You've seen me without a shirt before. At the tribal camp."

"I was too scared to care."

"But you care now?" he teased, draping his shirt across his bare shoulder.

Her eyes narrowed, and she worked hard to keep her gaze on his face.

He laughed, brushing past her as he headed toward the water. His mood had improved. Perhaps he was used to women who approved of half-dressed men parading about in front of them. Her thoughts pulled up short. Of course, in the Comanche camp of his teenage years, he probably ran around with even less body coverings.

Tawny skin rippled with each step, the muscles along his back were strong and lean. Heat moved from her cheeks to her neck. She turned away. Irritation grew—part of her annoyance directed at herself but much more at him. He would not toy with her. She expected more from him and intended to let him know.

When he returned a half-hour later, he was dressed. His hair lay damp against his head. A flash of white teeth shone as he smiled, irritating her all the more with his carefree demeanor.

"How is my father?" he asked.

"Resting and fine. The bleeding has subsided."

"Good. I'll check—"

"May I have a word with you before you go to him?"

He stopped in front of her. He stood a good foot taller than her, and his towering presence made her feel like a frail leaf dangling from a mighty oak.

"About?"

Her hand touched the lace upon her collar as her foolishness overwhelmed. With his father fighting for his life, did she really want to discuss his cavalier behavior? "Never mind, it can wait until later."

"You look upset. If I've done or said—"

She wished she could disappear. "No. It doesn't matter." She swished her hand through the air. "Please. Go check on your father."

"All right." He turned to walk away and then

stopped, looking back with a probing stare. "It's because I unbuttoned my shirt, isn't it?"

"No!" Her cheeks turned crimson. "Yes. But it's so unimportant now compared to everything else going on. I'm sorry I was bothered."

He moved close, taking her hands within his own. "And I'm sorry I teased you. I can assure you; no woman holds more of my respect right now than you do. You're the last person on earth I want to embarrass or hurt."

She blinked, not sure what to say. His apology left her feeling deflated. It seemed the more she got to know the man, the less she understood him. He dropped her hands, and she folded her arms. "Thank you."

He turned to walk away.

"Luke."

"Yes?"

"I'm curious. Why do I hold your respect?"

His hungry gaze drew the very breath from her lungs. "You've had your world turned upside down and look at you. You're still standing. I admire that in anyone—man or woman."

She nodded, pleased with his answer.

He turned away again, but she reached out, stopping him in his tracks. "Luke."

He grinned, his voice dipping several octaves. "Yes?"

"I admire you, too. You've stayed with me when most would have run for the hills. I know this isn't your fight, but still, your honor has kept you here."

"It is my fight, Billie. It's not just honor. It's also my job. I was hired by Littleton and Clark Detective Agency to bring in the person who stole property from the Justice City Bank, and I intend to finish what I started."

She was disappointed in his response. One part of her wanted to hear he was here because he had feelings for her, while another part never wanted to hear such words. It was absurd to think they could be more—a bounty hunter and a schoolteacher. Their worlds were too different.

His fingers that trembled slightly moved a lock of hair behind her ear.

She bit into her bottom lip—her gaze drawn to the ground between his feet. "Luke, I've not been candid with you."

"About?"

"I do find you attractive. That is the reason I want you to keep your distance. It would never work between us."

"Why? Because I'm part Comanche?"

"No." His assumption startled her. "Not at all. It's because of your work and my work. We're so different, and our worlds are night and day."

"You don't have to explain." His eyes held deep pain. "I understand."

"I don't think you do."

"More than you know," he snapped. "How would you introduce your half-breed beau to your parents? How would you introduce me to your friends? How would you introduce me to your students' parents?

How would you—"

"Stop behaving like such a goose!" She reached up on her tiptoes, wrapping her arms about his neck and pressing her lips against his in a fierce kiss.

His arms immediately encircled her slim waist, one moved against her spine and pulled her soft form against his own. He leaned into her, taking the kiss deeper until she felt sure she would faint.

Billie pulled back. "I'm sorry. I've never kissed a man before. I don't know what came over me."

He pulled her back into his arms, holding her tight against his chest. "Don't be sorry. I'm not."

Billie closed her eyes, nuzzling against his broad chest.

A groan sounded only feet away. Walking Stick.

Luke took her hand. "Come with me."

She intended to do just that—as long as she could. Maybe forever. Did she dare hope? Or was Luke like his father—a lone wolf who wanted the pleasure of a woman but on his terms? Her heart winced at the thought.

Lord, help me.

18

"Water…" Walking Stick spoke, his voice raspy.

Luke opened his canteen and poured small sips through the man's lips. He smoothed his hair back from his forehead then settled him back upon the soft blanket.

"Thank you."

He'd bled through the bandage again.

Billie didn't want to think about what Luke said about bleeding. She said another prayer as Luke unwrapped the wound, applied fresh salve, and then rewound the bandage about his father's broad chest.

"I am dying." Walking Stick's words sounded faint, like the whisper of water gliding over pebbles in a slow-moving stream.

"I'm not letting that happen," Luke replied.

The clouds had started to disappear, folded between the blanket of darkness that enveloped the evening.

Luke would soon make a fire to keep his father warm and any potential predators away.

"And when I go, I want a Christian burial." Walking Stick continued talking as if Luke had not spoken.

Luke leaned closer toward his father, his head almost on his chest as he looked him in the eyes. "Why are you talking like this?"

"A Christian burial is proper," Walking Stick said, though his voice sounded fainter. His eyelids lowered. "Your mother introduced me to the Lord many moons ago. I have strayed from the path, but like a deer panting for water, so I have returned."

"Don't talk so much," Luke said. "Save your strength."

Walking Stick closed his eyes, growing still.

"Dad?" Luke said, his voice filled with urgency even as his father lay limp.

Walking Stick opened his eyes and smiled.

It was the only time she'd seen such an expression on the man's blank features. Billie's palm moved to her chest, splayed across her heart. The older man closed his eyes once more, his smile fading into a peaceful rest.

Luke touched his father's wrist. "His pulse is weak."

"If you can catch another rabbit, I'll make some broth. It will help him regain his strength."

With only a nod, Luke slid dusty boots from his feet then disappeared with silent footsteps into the surroundings. Billie lay her hand upon Walking Stick's chest and prayed.

It was more than an hour later when Luke returned with a rabbit, already skinned and ready for boiling. She made the broth then passed the cup to Luke.

With a gentle hand, Luke spooned the liquid through his father's lips. Soon, the color returned to Walking Stick's cheeks and soft snores parted his lips.

"I don't believe God would bring my father back to me only to let him die," Luke said.

"Luke—" Part of her wanted to prepare him for what might come, but another part hesitated. Who was she to say what God would or would not do?

"Either way, I am thankful for this time with him," he said.

Either way. Those two words soothed Billie's soul. Luke would not make the same mistake he'd made with his mother. He would not turn from God or allow bitterness to take root. She was sure of it. Either way, his faith would sustain him.

Nightfall neared when Luke checked Walking Stick's bandage once more. His gaze shifted from his father's wound back to Billie. "Come look."

Billie inched closer, fearing what she might see. There was no fresh blood. Only a few specks of dark crimson from earlier in the day.

"The bleeding has stopped," he said.

"Can't you let an old man rest?" Walking Stick grumbled, rolling onto his side.

Billie's hope soared. "Complaining is always a good sign."

Luke grinned, leaning back against a tree trunk. "He will live to complain another day. I'm sure of it."

Silent praises poured from her being. *Oh, yes, Lord, let it be so!*

~*~

Several days rolled by and Walking Stick grew stronger with each passing hour. He had insisted on taking a walk so he could enjoy solitude and commune with God. Although resistant at first, Luke left his father alone to do as he wished.

Luke stood near a grove of trees with leafy boughs as he watched him meander off. "I think my father is well enough to travel now. He asked me to journey with him to visit Abigail and her family."

She stood at his side, trying to ignore the crushing within her chest. Was he about to send her to Arkansas alone? Words she never intended to say spilled forth. "I'm not ready to say good-bye. I need more time."

His knuckles stroked her jawline while his gaze held hers in a tender embrace. "How will your aunt and uncle feel about a tribal Comanche in their home?" When she didn't answer, he continued. "I can't leave him. He won't survive on his own."

Billie wanted to offer him assurance. "It has been many years since I've seen my aunt and uncle. I only know they were always kind to me, and I would expect them to show kindness to you and your father."

He reached out, pulled her into his arms, and kissed her head before turning away. She wasn't sure he was convinced, but he didn't question her.

Very soon he would leave her in Arkansas and never return. Silent tears fell. She would not let Luke see her sorrow. She needed her to remain steady and strong at his side. His shoulders already carried so much. She would not add her selfish burdens to the heavy weight. A bittersweet ache filled her being.

She truly looked forward to seeing Aunt Matilda. It had been at least eight years since she had spent time with her and Uncle Rupert. Yet the reality of her situation with Luke kept her heart from fully experiencing gladness. Just like White Feather, what she wanted would never be.

Luke Lancaster had lived his life by the gun and wandering the plains.

How could she dare hope for anything different?

~*~

The next three days brought a subdued mood that would not relinquish its hold — much like the overcast sky. Drops of rain fell the entire time, typically soft and gentle, but sometimes so hard they had to wait patiently under tree branches for a reprieve.

The trio traveled slow. Every few hours, they stopped so Luke could check his father's bandages. The wound never bled, and for that, he thanked God.

His father rode on Billie's horse. She rode sideways in front of Luke, nestled between his arms. The scent of her inflamed his senses and the softness of her chaffed his soul. This woman had ignited something within his being that he'd long thought buried. Could he really just ride away from her? Never think of her again? Or would every waking and sleeping moment remind him of what might have been?

He'd come to have deep affection for Billie—they'd been through hardship and laughter together and formed a bond he wasn't ready to break. He wanted to ask her if he could come back for her but knew that only meant one thing: marriage. How could he marry, and then leave a wife to worry about him while he went about capturing outlaws on the run?

No one deserved that worry. Billie said it herself. Their lives were too different. She had her profession and wouldn't want to stop teaching. He had his job and needed a couple more years of saving money before he could stop. So, what was there to do?

He glanced over his shoulder and caught his father gazing longingly up into the hills. A blanket of greenery hung about the mountainside—vines and tree branches tangled together to create a beautiful scene. It reminded him of a magnificent curtain he'd once seen at an opera house—thick and heavy. But this one shimmered beneath the sprinkle of rain, making it even more breathtaking.

A town sat perched high—quaint houses built upon rocks and a white-washed church with a tall steeple taking center stage. It was picturesque and pristine—the type of place Billie deserved to live.

He inhaled the crisp air. Arkansas was more than he expected. He was sorry he hadn't come sooner.

She pointed upward. "I remember my Aunt Matilda saying how they built the town up high because when the spring rains come, the water washes away everything in the lowland."

"It's beautiful here," Walking Stick said, inhaling

deeply.

She smiled. "Yes, but I'll always miss my home."

"This is only temporary," Luke said, half-believing his own words. "Until we can clear your name."

"That could take months, couldn't it?" she asked.

"Yes, or it might only take weeks."

"Or, I might always be wanted."

"I don't intend to let that happen."

As if sensing more needed to be said, Walking Stick tugged on the reins to the horse, nudging the mare toward higher ground and giving them privacy.

Billie Jo lay her head against his chest. "I'll miss you."

"Billie Jo, I'm—"

"Yes?"

"I'm not willing to just ride away and never see you again." His knuckles tightened around the reins. "I don't know what I have to offer you, but—"

She lifted her head and met his gaze, causing him to stumble over his thoughts. What was he thinking anyway? Was he considering asking her to wait for him for a few years while he worked on his plan for the future—while he finished his to-do list? How was that even fair? Only a selfish man would make such a proposal, and he wouldn't be selfish.

"Yes?"

"It doesn't matter."

"It might matter to me."

The sound of church bells ringing in the distance stopped them. The sweet melody rang throughout the green valley, echoing off the majestic mountainside and brought a smile to Billie's face.

Luke grinned at her. "Looks as if we've arrived in time for church."

19

Billie gazed up at the stately house. She slid out of the saddle and onto solid ground. "I think this is the place. Best I can remember."

Luke joined her, taking in the formidable structure. It was two stories, sprawling with a wraparound porch, a balcony for the upstairs bedrooms, multiple gables, and fine detailing on the handrails and around the windows. Several chimneys jutted upward from different sides of the structure, and two columns guided visitors and family members toward the large oak entry door.

Walking Stick remained in the saddle. A tense expression covered his features. She knew he was not used to riding through towns. Years of being a loner had left him content with wide open spaces.

"My Uncle Rupert owns a sawmill. It belonged to his father before him. He's done quite well for himself."

"So I see," Luke said.

"His first wife died in childbirth along with the child. When he married my aunt, she was already in her thirties with him in his forties."

"Did they ever have any children?"

She shook her head, sorrow welling up within her bosom. She'd heard of the tears her aunt had cried, desiring a child more than her next breath. It never happened, but her husband devoted himself to her—giving her happiness above his own. "Last I heard, they volunteered at the local orphanage and gave funds to provide a proper education to all the children there."

"As a teacher, I'm sure you find that a good thing," Walking Stick said.

She smiled. "Yes, and an educated child grows into a productive member of society. That benefits us all."

The door creaked open. The older woman who stared back could not have looked more different than her aunt. Her hair was brunette, with streaks of gray, and she was as round as a pumpkin. Her gaze darted about their faces. A hint of nervousness lingered upon her expression. "May I help you?".

"I'm sorry." Billie's cheeks warmed "I thought this was the home of Matilda and Rupert Schumann."

"It was, until about a month ago," the woman said. "Now they live outside of town. Just follow this road. It'll take you to the Schumann Ranch."

"Did you say a ranch?" That did not make sense. Her Uncle Rupert was too old to work a ranch.

"Yes. A very nice ranch." She smiled, her anxiety easing. "Matilda would not settle for anything less, and even if she would, well, Rupert wouldn't allow it."

That certainly sounded like her relatives, but there'd been no mention about them moving. Matilda had always said this was her forever home.

"I'm surprised, with their age and all." Then, feeling awkward, she added, "I'm their niece, but it's been about eight years since I've seen either of them. They weren't all that young then, and—"

"Oh, they have plenty of help," the woman said. "But perhaps I've said too much. The Schumanns are good folk. I'll let them tell their own business. I don't want to be known as the town gossip." She glanced past Billie, looking where the horses nibbled on blades of grass. Her gaze bounced from Luke and then to his father. "Would you like a drink of water or to feed your horses before you go on down the road?"

"No need," Luke spoke up. "We refreshed them right before we came into town, but thank you for your hospitality."

In less than an hour, they stood at a gate with a sign that read, "Schumann Ranch & Boys' Home." The fence stretched as far as she could see, encompassing acres of rolling hills and several ponds. Cattle roamed about the pasture while a dozen or so horses gathered around a fenced-off area.

Off in the distance sat a large log cabin. Trees surrounded one end of the structure. The other end held a balcony that opened up toward the hills.

"This isn't at all what I expected," Billie said.

"Do you still want to stay?"

Where was there to go? "I think I do. If they'll have me."

"Then let's go find out." He clicked his tongue, and his horse began to move down the dirt path that led to the log cabin.

Surely, her aunt and uncle wouldn't turn her away? But if they had a boys' ranch, they might think twice. Rupert would not want to put anyone in jeopardy. He was logical like that. Matilda would throw caution to the wind, but she was known for being impetuous, or so her mother had said.

She decided not to fret about something she could not control. She would tell the entire truth. What happened after that was in God's hands. Whether she stayed or left, He was with her.

~*~

Luke knocked on the door. Feet shuffled.

A muffled voice sounded from behind the door. Finally, a lanky young man who appeared to be in his early teens, with freckled cheeks and round brown eyes, answered the door.

"Good afternoon." Billie paused for several seconds, a mask of confusion across her features. "We're here to see Rupert and Matilda Schumann. Is this the right place?"

"Who wants to know?"

"I'm her niece. And you are?"

"I just live here. Freddy's my name. Come in."

Somewhat hesitantly, Billie stepped inside.

Luke followed her then Walking Stick.

Bunkbeds filled the room, lining the walls. Almost twenty young men—different sizes, shapes, races, and ages stared back at them with curious eyes.

The freckled boy lifted his chin and smiled. "And here's all my brothers."

The boys waved. Some sat on the bed, reading a book. Others played checkers at a nearby table. Another group snapped peas into bowls. Not one soul seemed to notice or care that a Comanche stood in their midst. She could only reason it was because they were all so different, such things had ceased to matter to them.

"We don't do much work on Sunday," Freddy said. "The Schumanns don't allow it. They said all we need to do is go to church and rest, so we'll be ready to work again come Monday."

"I see. And, where are the Schumanns?" Billie asked.

"Their house is just behind this one. I'll show you the way."

He gave them a quick, follow-me wave then headed out the door with fast footsteps.

Billie had to double-time to keep up. Luke had no trouble with his long legs. Walking Stick moved slow, still appearing anxious despite the warm welcome.

The house behind the large log cabin was smaller and looked recently built if the fresh condition of the logs was any indication.

"I'll leave you to get reacquainted," Freddy said. "Guessin' I'll see you all tomorrow?"

"Yes, I hope so."

He smiled and then walked back the way he came.

Billie could barely breathe from sudden fear. What if they turned her away? What if no one cared that she'd traveled all this distance? What if they were too elderly to put up with the thought of any trouble and told her to skedaddle?

"What are you waiting on? Go ahead and knock," Luke said.

"What if they don't want me here?"

"Of course, they'll want you here. You're their niece."

"I suppose you're right." Her hand rose to her stomach. "It's just been so odd, trying to get to this door. First, we went to the wrong house, then the wrong house again. How can I be sure this is the right one? How can I be sure this is what God wants?"

Luke laughed as he reached around her and knocked on the door.

Startled, she held still as a statue until Rupert answered the door.

He looked momentarily confused, a bushy gray brow dipping downward.

"Uncle Rupert. I'm Billie Jo—"

The elderly man grinned. "It can't be... Billie Jo barely came up past my ribs. You're a grown woman, and a pretty one, to boot."

"It's me, Uncle Rupert." Billie noted that Luke looked mighty pleased. Of course, he would. Now, he could leave in peace—trusting she was safe with those who loved her. She just wished he didn't look so happy about it. She held out her hand as if carrying a platter. "And this is my traveling companion, Mr. Lancaster."

Luke's smile vanished, and for a moment, she was

glad.

"And his father, and my friend, Walking Stick."

Rupert took a step back then opened his door wider. "Welcome."

20

Billie looked around her. The inside of the cabin displayed colorful furnishings and bright cups mixed in with books in cases along one wall.

"I may not have a fancy town home," Matilda began with a twinkle in her eye. "But I insisted upon some luxuries—my teacups from Paris and my silk bedspread from Patna."

Aunt Matilda wore a plain mauve dress with no frills except a small opal brooch. She was far from the sophisticated and glamorous older sister her mother had spoken of with a hint of envy. Now, her beauty was subdued—laced with streaks of gray, fine lines, and a winsome smile. "We've given up the social life for one that is far more rewarding."

"The boys?" Billie guessed. She sat directly across from her aunt on a settee. Luke sat next to her, squirming a bit and seeming uncomfortable on the small piece of furniture. Matilda and Uncle Rupert sat in chairs, a small table between them for their cups. Walking Stick stood near the door, leaning against the frame with arms crossed and insisting he'd had enough sitting.

"Yes, the boys," Rupert said, adding a chuckle.

"We knew the Lord wanted us to have children. We just never knew he wanted us to have so many."

"How long have you had the ranch? Mother never mentioned it."

"I've not told a soul. It just felt too much like bragging."

Rupert's gentle voice flowed with humility. "We've had the ranch operational for about three years now. We only moved into this house a month or so ago. Until then, we had a married couple living inside the cabin with the boys. They kept an eye on them and made sure they did what was expected. The couple took off for California—said the Lord called them as missionaries to the miners. So, here we are, doing the best we can."

Billie nodded, intrigued to hear more about the ranch and its day-to-day operations.

"What's expected?" Luke asked, his question somewhat biting.

"Excuse me?" Rupert gave Luke a hard stare.

"Most of them look young." Luke's tone softened. "I'm curious what is expected of them?"

"We expect them to carry their weight. This is a fully functioning ranch. The boys get up early. Do chores, such as animal watering and feeding, fence mending, cattle branding, and the like. It doesn't take all day. They are usually finished by late afternoon, giving them plenty of time to rest and do their studies before supper. After that, they're free to do what they wish until bedtime."

"Who is their teacher?" Billie asked.

"I am," Matilda said. "Though I'm not that good at it. I've forgotten so much. Perhaps you—?"

Something sprang to life within Billie's being. She had to remind herself to keep calm and think—not jump at an opportunity that might or might not be the Lord's will.

"I should not presume so much, dear." Aunt Matilda reached over to pat her hand. "We're so excited you've come. We never get to see family. Though I don't know how long you intend to stay..."

"You're welcomed here as long as you'd like." Uncle Rupert added. "Matilda gets lonely without any female companionship." He gave Billie a quick wink. "I try to fill the void, but I don't know much about cross-stitching or baking mincemeat pies or how to make soap."

Billie looked at Luke. His expression had turned grave. She turned back to her aunt and uncle. "Perhaps I should explain why I'm here." Her throat tightened—constricted by the dread of what she was about to say. A silent prayer moved through her thoughts.

Lord Jesus, if You would strengthen me in my inner being, giving me the courage to say what needs to be said and the wisdom to know how to say it. Let Your hand guide this entire situation and replace any hesitation or worry I have with Your peace—the peace that passes all understanding.

Luke's hand moved toward hers, laying across her knuckles to give her a reassuring pat before sliding away.

"Is something wrong?" Aunt Matilda asked. "Is

everything all right at home? I know your mother has experienced more than her share of heartache over this past year."

Billie regrouped, gaining her strength and starting again. "Yes, my parents have endured trial after trial this year, but God has remained faithful and ministered to them."

"Then what?" Aunt Matilda asked, her voice quivering.

"It's me, Aunt Matilda," Billie began. "I'm accused of murder, but I assure you, I'm innocent."

"Murder?" Aunt Matilda blinked, her frail hand rising to her bosom. "Did you say murder?"

"Of course, you're innocent," Uncle Rupert exclaimed, puffing out his chest as if outraged.

"You would never—" Aunt Matilda began.

"I've been framed by a man who stole money from his own bank," Billie began. "He took small amounts of gold from the miners over several months and adjusted deposit slips to hide his thieving. An employee at the bank, and a good friend of mine, uncovered his crime. He was going to report him, and—" Billie's heart beat wildly in her chest.

"Instead, the owner of the bank had him killed," Luke interjected. "He intended to kill Billie Jo, but she escaped."

"Oh, my…" Aunt Matilda's pale cheeks turned ghostly white.

"Now, the man who orchestrated the robbery and the murder is after Billie," Luke continued. "He wants her dead because she knows the truth."

"Yes. And while the man's posse appears to have lost our trail, there's no guarantee they won't come after me. If I stay here, there's a possibility of danger."

"You are family," Uncle Rupert said. "You will stay here. As long as you like."

"Oh yes, dear." Aunt Matilda nodded. "It's probably one of the safest places you could be."

Uncle Rupert's gaze shifted toward Luke and then to Walking Stick. "You're welcomed to stay, too, if you'd like. We can always use extra hands with the ranch and someone who can help show these young men what it's like to do honest work."

"Thank you," Walking Stick said, the edges of his lips lifting. "For welcoming me into your home. The work you do here is of the Lord, and one day, I will return. I will teach your young men how to track and hunt and make arrows. But now, I must go to my daughter—a daughter I have only known from afar."

"I intend to go with him," Luke said. "Then take care of some unfinished business."

"Luke saved my life," Billie said, giving him a fond gaze and then glancing away. "He's going back to El Paso then on to Justice City to capture the true criminals."

"A person of principle." Uncle Rupert lifted his chin with a gleam of pride. "I admire that in a man."

"It's what I was hired to do," Luke said. "I work for Littleton and Clark Detective Agency as a recovery specialist. That's just a fancy phrase for bounty hunter."

Aunt Matilda's face paled. Her hand rose to her

bosom where she fumbled with her broach. "I see…"

"It's not as bad as it sounds. He has never killed a soul. He always brings the outlaws in alive." Billie hoped they believed her.

Darkness had moved upward and over Luke's features.

"Let's not get into that." Uncle Rupert's brows were drawn together, but his eyes were kind. "You know how your aunt feels about guns."

"What Luke does is no different than what a sheriff would do," Billie's tone was tart.

"Perhaps so…" Aunt Matilda began, her hands trembling in her lap.

Tension crawled up Billie's spine. Walking Stick's relaxed stance had now turned anxious—his spine stiff and legs slightly spread. Luke frowned, and his jaw clenched. She had to diffuse the situation before it was too late.

"I know what you're thinking," Billie continued. "I used to think the same way—that bounty hunters are hired guns. But that's not the case. They catch criminals. It's a service to society."

Aunt Matilda pressed her lips closed.

"Of course, it is," Uncle Rupert said, turning to Luke. "How good of a shot are you?"

"Rupert!" Aunt Matilda exclaimed. "Do you forget we have a cabin full of boys here? We do not need to fill their minds with visions of gun-slinging."

Billie's mouth opened to defend Luke, but he didn't give her a chance.

He rose, dropping his hat back upon his head.

"Perhaps I should go."

"No, please." Aunt Matilda began. "I didn't mean that the way it sounded."

"It's quite all right. I'm used to it."

Uncle Rupert stood up. "We would like you to stay. You saved our niece's life. That means more than what you do for a living."

Billie cringed. The situation was growing worse by the second. She stood up, looking him square in the face. "Luke, please don't go. Not yet. I'm not ready—"

Coldness permeated every syllable he spoke. "There's never a good time to separate paths, is there?"

Billie's heart fell. She knew that look—the distance that pushed her away and most likely protected his heart at the same time. "You are coming back, aren't you?"

His eyes remained steadfast though sorrow seemed to linger barely beyond his gaze. "I'll send someone to let you know the outcome."

"But I—" Crushing pain stopped any words. Tears clung to the edge of her lashes. She no longer cared what Luke or anyone else thought of her—whether they believed her weak, brave, brazen, or anything at all. She only knew she did not want him to leave. It was too soon. She needed time to adjust—time to mentally prepare for the inevitable.

Aunt Matilda stood with difficulty and reached for a cane. "I never intended to cause harm. Please do not leave, Mr. Lancaster. This is all my fault. I'm afraid of guns, but only because I accidentally shot myself in the foot when I was a young girl. I do appreciate all you've done for our niece."

"That's quite all right." He gave her a gentle smile. "You've probably helped move a situation along that was bound to happen. I can't stay, and Billie needs to stay, so we have little choice in the matter." He glanced from Aunt Matilda to Uncle Rupert. "Thank you for the refreshment."

Walking Stick bobbed his head in a silent good-bye, a look of regret fastening upon Billie before he disappeared out the door. Luke strode toward the exit with sure footsteps, intending to follow after his father.

"Luke Lancaster." Billie rushed toward him, standing only inches away, anger permeating the air. "After all we've been through together, I would think a proper farewell is the least you can give me."

Uncle Rupert motioned his wife back to her chair. He sat down in his own, nodding toward the door. "The porch will afford you more privacy."

They'd barely stepped outside together before Billie fell into Luke's arms. Walking Stick had disappeared, but that would not have stopped her. Her clenched fist rested on his chest even as hot tears rolled down her cheeks. How could he! How could he leave her so easily? Had she ever mattered to him?

"Stop that," Luke whispered into her hair, wrapping his arms around her and squeezing her against his hard chest. "You know I can't stay."

"Why not?" She stepped back, looking at him without bothering to hide her longing. "We could get married, and you and I could build a house nearby. My aunt and uncle might even let us stay here and help at the ranch."

"And have you defend me for the rest of our lives?" He shook his head. "No, thank you."

"I don't care about that. I'd defend you to the entire world."

"You probably would," he said, adding a tender grin. "But at what cost?"

"You sound like your father."

He winced.

"Instead of asking me all the questions, perhaps you should ask yourself one or two." she began. "What is the cost of leaving? Are you willing to pay that price?"

"I'll clear your name. Did you forget that part of this puzzle?"

"Forget clearing my name. Let them think what they will. I know the truth; you know the truth, and God knows the truth."

He took a step backward, his palms cupping her elbows. "But it's not fair to your murdered friend if we let Clovis Caldwell or Sheriff McGregor get away with their crime. Where's the justice for Malcolm?"

Her entire body rose and fell in smooth upheaval. How could she argue with that logic? Malcolm deserved justice. If it meant she would lose Luke in the process, perhaps that was her due for leading her friend to make the wrong decision.

He dropped his hand then moved a stray tendril away from her face. She could feel his anguish as surely as it was her own. His eyes lowered to her lips, but he stepped away. "I've got to go into town while it's still light. I need to refresh my supplies." He stepped off the porch, moving toward his horse. "I'll be gone tonight."

She nodded, knowing there was nothing else she could say. He was already gone, miles away in his mind but forever nearby in her heart.

21

The young men and boys at the ranch gravitated toward Billie—drawn by her compassion toward them and the discipline they craved. With Uncle Rupert's help, she purchased a desk and brought it into the room with the bunk beds. The boys moved the beds closer to the opposite end of the cabin then hung a sheet to partition off the classroom area.

It was far from perfect, but it would do for now. Eventually she hoped a separate schoolhouse could be added to the property.

As it turned out, Freddy was very helpful and appeared to be a leader—in part because he was the oldest but also because he knew how to do the most. She never asked any of the boys their circumstances or how they became orphaned. Instead, she devoted herself to preparing lessons and doing what she loved to do—*teach*.

She'd not heard a word from Luke after he said good-bye to her on the front porch. Already, several weeks had passed. Far too often, it felt like yesterday. When she thought of Luke, every emotion remained raw and painful—a fresh wound that refused to heal.

Her heart hurt, and the tears flowed when she

found herself alone, but that only served to make her more determined to work hard and pray more. Work and prayer seemed to bring the only relief.

Her Aunt Matilda needed help getting around—suffering terribly with an arthritic hip. At first, Billie only assisted her aunt in making the meals, but she soon found herself recruiting a couple of the young men to cook with her so they could relieve Aunt Matilda of the entire responsibility.

More than once, Aunt Matilda apologized for upsetting Billie's "beau," but Billie consoled her by telling her that God could turn the situation around if He saw fit.

Uncle Rupert appeared especially pleased with the fact she had taken on the organization of the meals. He wanted her to stay on. Over coffee one morning, while Aunt Matilda still rested and the boys had yet to awaken, he'd tried to convince her.

"The room is yours for as long as you'd like," Uncle Rupert said. "It may be small, but you can call it your own."

Billie tapped the top of her half-full coffee cup with her index finger. "I thought you wanted to save the room—in case Aunt Matilda ever needed a fulltime nurse."

"She's much better," he said. "Now that you've taken over the meals and relieved her of so much standing. I've even heard her laugh a time or two, so I know she's improving."

"I don't know," Billie said with an inward groan as she maneuvered toward the hot stove. "I always hoped I'd go back to Justice City with my parents and my students."

"You have students right here."

"I do enjoy it here. I feel useful. And the boys are eager to learn. That brings joy to my heart."

"You're not only useful, Billie," he said. "You're needed. Please stay."

She reached over and took a rag, wrapping it about the coffeepot handle and pouring another cup for her uncle. "I should pray about it, and so should you."

"One day, your aunt and I will no longer be able to run this place. It would be good if we could leave it to a family member who loves the work and could oversee the operation."

"The entire operation?" She set the coffeepot down with a thud. "I can only cook and teach. I know nothing about cattle and those sorts of things."

"Perhaps you'll marry someone who does." He took a slow sip of his coffee. "Until then, you have Freddy. He might not know much yet, but he's learning more every day. He's only a fourteen-year-old kid, but in a few years, he'll be a big help."

"Well, marriage is out of the question. So, Freddy had better learn fast."

"Are you happy here, Billie?" He asked. "Because this conversation is a waste of time if you're not happy here."

"I am comfortable," she answered in truth. Happiness had walked out the door with Luke, but this was a good life. She felt tremendous gratitude toward her relatives, even though she did not often speak of it. She was not living in caves, nursing bullet wounds, or running for her life disguised as a man. God had kept her safe and brought her to this place. How could she complain? "You've opened your home to me and given me more than I dared hope. I am very grateful to you, Aunt Matilda, and the Lord. This life fits me, so I would say that I am comfortable."

"But something is missing?"

"There is nothing you can do about that." She glanced away to blink back the tears.

"Is it your beau?"

"I should push him out of my mind like he has pushed me out of his mind."

Uncle Rupert chuckled. "How can you be so sure he won't come back for you?"

"I can't think about it. I've got meals to cook and students to teach." She folded her arms. "And so what if he does come back? That doesn't mean anything—not really. He walked out and left me. That's what matters most."

"Is that why you stay so busy? You don't have time to think about what might've been?"

Her hands dropped to her side. "I should start gathering eggs…"

"A man doesn't stay beside a woman like Luke stayed by you unless he cares a great deal about her. I dare to say, he might even love her."

Billie froze, her gaze locked upon the wooden floorboards. His words sent an arrow slicing into her heart. If he only knew how much it hurt to contemplate such a thing—to consider the possibility that she'd let love slip between her fingers. What could she have done differently? How could she have convinced him to stay? Luke was gone, and a wise woman would let him go.

Uncle Rupert leaned back in his chair. "Just thought you might want to know."

There was one thing Uncle Rupert didn't know, but she did. Luke had wanderlust in his veins. Until that changed, no woman would claim his heart.

"Thank you." Billie offered up a faint smile, wanting the conversation to cease. "I'll be back soon and start breakfast."

~*~

Luke's shrill whistle ricocheted about the countryside.

Walking Stick drew the horse to a sudden stop, staring at his son. "Why did you do that?"

"Your daughter is a better shot than most men. I don't want to surprise her."

He reached up, wiping faint beads of sweat off his forehead and then down his deerskin pants. "I'm not sure this is a good plan. Perhaps I should have sent you ahead, to prepare her."

"You're not nervous, are you?" Luke asked, trying not to chuckle.

"I have only seen Abigail from afar. What if—"

"You know what my mother always said?"

Walking Stick nodded. "She said what ifs were

faith in worry, not faith in God."

From the distance, Abigail appeared on the porch. A man stood with her, holding a child.

"Abigail has a heart like our mother. She won't turn you away." He hoped and prayed he told the truth. Abigail could be unpredictable at times.

Walking Stick clicked the reins, moving in slow motion. Luke kept pace, not trying to lead, but letting his father guide them forward. Though he never said the words, he was proud of his father—proud that he wanted restoration and a renewed relationship with his children. His only regret was that his mother was not alive to see the miracle.

They were still quite a distance away when Abigail stepped from the porch. Her hand rose to lay across her bosom as she stepped forward.

"She is beautiful, like your mother," Walking Stick whispered.

Abigail lifted her skirts above her ankles and ran out to meet them. Several strands of hair tumbled about her shoulders and her breath came in ragged gasps. *She knew.* Luke could see it in her eyes. Without a word being spoken, she knew Walking Stick was their father.

Without a second of hesitation, Walking Stick slid from his horse. She rushed into his arms, tears wetting her cheeks. Luke watched in silent gratitude.

After several seconds Abigail loosened her grip and looked up at Luke in brown-eyed amazement. "How?"

"How?" Luke pointed upward. "That's how. Now,

can two weary travelers get a fresh drink of water, or have you forgotten how to treat guests?"

"I don't care about water," Walking Stick said. "I want to meet my grandson. I already know he has lungs like a wolf."

"How can you know that?" Abigail said, her face washed in confusion.

"There is much we need to talk about," Luke said.

"I also want to see your mother's grave," Walking Stick said, surprising them both. "I have a few words I need to say."

"What can you say to her? She's not there. It's just bones," Luke said.

Abigail's gentle expression turned toward her father. "We do not believe in a happy hunting ground. We believe her spirit is with the Lord."

"I believe, as well. My words are to Him, not to her."

22

It was two hours later before Abigail and Luke showed their father where their mother was laid to rest. It was on several acres of land surrounded by mesquite with a naturally flowing stream nearby. The burnt rubble of a house still remained, though much of the wood had rotted or floated away in gray ash. It was a sight that still hurt Luke's heart.

"We buried her here, on her land. It was what she would've wanted," he said.

Walking Stick stood silent as he stared at the single white cross only feet away.

Henry, Sr., stood beside his wife, his arm draped across her shoulder. Abigail had already told them she was expecting again. That explained the glow upon her cheeks and the quiet beauty that surrounded her like a delicate veil.

A deep voice began to speak toward heaven as Walking Stick lifted his gaze upward. "Father God, You have brought Your son home. You have given me more than I deserve. I thank You for all You have done, and I ask You to forgive me for a past I cannot undo. Let me be the son You want me to be, from this day forward, and forevermore."

Luke squatted down and touched the ground at his feet. Heat seared his eyes as a release rolled from his innermost being. Anger and regret flowed from his soul, cleansing him in a gentle current of grace. No one spoke. They let silence do its work, until Henry, Jr., began to whimper.

"I'm sure he's hungry and tired," Abigail said.

"We should head back." Henry, Sr., patted her shoulder.

"We'll go with you," Luke said, glancing toward his father. "We've got to go to El Paso for business."

Walking Stick lifted his hand upward, drawing their attention. Luke knew it was the way he'd done before speaking in the tribal council. It meant his words held weight.

"I want to stay here," he said.

"Since when do you stay anywhere?" Luke asked in confusion.

"Since today."

"With us?" Abigail asked, hope upon her features.

Walking Stick made a slow circle. "Where I should have stayed all along. At this place. On this land."

Abigail looked to Luke.

He nodded in approval. "Then consider it yours. But what happened to the lone wolf?"

"My soul has found its rest. I am no longer searching."

Abigail reached out, placing her hand in her father's and laying her head upon his shoulder. Just the sight warmed Luke's heart. His father would get to see Abigail often—probably more often than he wanted. He'd also get to know Henry, Sr., and come to admire his quiet wisdom. He'd get to watch Henry, Jr., grow into a man and even teach him how to make arrowheads and string a bow. And he'd have a chance to be part of a family. Not just any family, but his own. He knew it was exactly what his mother would want.

The thought brought sweetness to his soul and clarity to his vision. Confusion and doubt vanished. He knew what he had to do. Like his father, he was no longer searching. He had found his home—with Billie.

~*~

Luke sat in Theo's office. "Your man hasn't come up with anything?"

"Sheriff McGregor is slicker than you think." Theo twisted the tips of his mustache—first one side then the other. "Our man says he never lets his guard down and looks as clean as the Rocky Mountain snow. He won't take a drop of liquor, so there's no chance of loosening his lips. Our man's starting to think McGregor is innocent, and we're barking up the wrong tree."

"And you? What do you think?"

"I'm still on your side. But we've got to prove you're right—preferably before your friend ends up dead."

"I have her hidden away."

"Where is she?" Theo asked.

Luke eyed him suspiciously. "Why do you want to know?"

Theo shook his head, not bothering to hide his

growing annoyance. "All right. Keep your secrets. But is she safe?"

"For now. Don't act so offended. At this point, I don't trust my own shadow. I'm keeping Billie Jo's whereabouts to myself."

"We need more time. Suspects always crack. I've learned that criminals like to brag. Our guy will eventually get him to talk."

Luke shook his head. "No, Theo. I appreciate your help on this one, but I've got a new plan."

"How about you share it with me since Littleton and Clark is the one who hired you, and I'm the director of this operation?"

"I'd rather not."

"Did you forget that I'm the one who pays you?"

"You've never interfered in my plans before," Luke said, working to keep his temper. "Why would you want to start now?"

Theo held up his hands in resignation. "Very well. Do what you need to do, but the insurance company wants someone to blame for taking their money. They're not paying until there's an arrest, which means we won't get paid either. So whatever you do—"

"It all comes down to money, doesn't it?" Luke shook his head, a smirk upon his lips. "You don't care who gets arrested as long as someone does."

"I don't know what's got you all twisted up, but that's not even close to the truth." Theo thumped his desktop with his finger. "I want the person responsible for the murder of Malcolm Jones and the stolen gold to be caught and sentenced. That's what I want." He straightened his back, his stare unflinching. "Now, I'd appreciate an apology."

Luke sank back into the chair with an exhale.

Theo loosened his stiff spine, leaning forward with a kinder gaze. "Must be woman troubles. Nothing messes with a man's head like a woman."

Luke growled under his breath. "My personal life is none of your business."

"It is if it affects your job."

"Maybe so, but I'm about done with this line of work. After this assignment, I'm doing something different with my life."

Theo gaped. "You can't be serious."

"I'm every bit of serious. It's getting harder to tell the good guys from the bad guys. When I first started, I felt as if I was doing something positive. Now, I'm not so sure."

"You're our most trusted recovery specialist."

Luke hesitated for several seconds, staring out across the room and the busyness that continued within them. The hectic pace of life. The faces that changed every week. The demands of a job that took a toll on the human existence. It was getting more difficult every day.

Was it because of Billie Jo? In part, he admitted. But she wasn't the only reason. When he took the time to examine his life, there was more—more reasons to rethink his goals and decide where he wanted to spend his future, and with whom.

She'd been right about his father. Walking Stick had made the wrong choice when he'd left his family behind, walking away from those who loved him the most. He didn't want to make that same mistake. He didn't want to look in the mirror and see the face of regret. If ever there was a time to rethink his life, the time was now.

"You're going after her, aren't you? You've fallen in love with Billie Jo Batson." When Luke didn't respond, Theo sighed—a heavy sound that drew his shoulders upward then down in one fluid movement. "Luke. We need you."

"Maybe. But someone I love needs me more." Luke's heart pounded as he said the words. He loved her. It was an admission that filled him with joy...and fear. Would she forgive him enough to take him back?

"I hope she's worth it. You're walking away from a lucrative way of life—a job most men only wish they could have. If you need more money—"

Luke stood up. "She's worth it—and no, I don't need more money." That wasn't entirely true. He didn't have enough to purchase a spread like he wanted, but if he could convince Billie Jo to be part of his life, he'd settle on a smaller place.

"All right, then." Theo rose, extending his hand. "One last job. Let's make it a good one."

23

The early morning sun shone upon the small house with fresh paint and yellow curtains. Chickens pecked about the yard. A rooster stood nearby, giving him a scrutinizing eye. An arrow-shaped weathervane twirled about the roof. All and all, the house seemed well maintained but ordinary.

Luke made his way up the steps to the wrap-around porch. Boards creaked beneath his weight. He'd barely finished knocking when an attractive older woman stood at the door. She wiped her hands upon a white apron and giving him a blank stare. "Hello?"

His eyes lingered upon copper hair streaked with gray. "Good morning. My name is Luke Lancaster, and I'm a friend of Billie Jo's. Are you Mrs. Batson?"

"Yes …" She straightened and her features twisted in turmoil. "I'm sorry, but Billie is not here. I'm not sure where she might be at the moment."

"I know where she is, ma'am."

A faint light flickered across her gaze. He knew that look. It was one of hope. "You've talked to her?"

"Billie Jo wants you to know that she's safe."

"Oh, my …" Mrs. Batson's hand lifted to her chest as she opened the door. "Come in. Please."

He stepped inside, noting the neatness of the house and the sweet smell of peaches and cinnamon that permeated the air. She led him down the hallway toward the dining area, where she removed a kettle of boiling water from the stovetop. "I was about to do the dishes. I'm sorry I don't have anything to feed you at the moment, but if you can stay a bit, I've got peach cobbler baking."

"I can't stay. Billie Jo told me it wouldn't be safe."

"No. I suppose not." Thin shoulders slumped in disappointment. "How is she doing? Is she well? Where has she gone?"

He grinned. "How about we take one question at a time."

"I'm so relieved." Her blue eyes gleamed. "I thought I'd never see her again. I thought—well, I'm sure you know what I thought."

"You look a little pale. Do you want to sit down?"

"I'm fine." She reached out, placing her hand on the back of a chair to keep steady. "Just so relieved—"

"Billie Jo is doing well. Yes, she is safe, and I'm not telling anyone where she's staying. I'm sure you'll learn soon enough."

"And what was your name?"

"Luke Lancaster. I'm determined to clear your daughter's name. I know she's innocent. Any prayers you can spare would be appreciated."

A frail hand reached out, touching his forearm. "Billie is my only living daughter, Mr. Lancaster. Her older sister died in childbirth. It has been so hard not knowing." Tears clung to the tips of pale lashes. "I can't tell you how much this means to my husband and me. He's in town buying a few supplies, but I know he'll be excited to hear you came to visit."

"Does he go to town often?"

"Every week." Her brows dipped in confusion. "It's not very far."

Luke reached inside his pocket and pulled out a wad of bills, smoothing them out, and then handing them to her. "Billie Jo was worried about a horse she'd *borrowed* from the livery stable when she escaped. Would you please take this money to the stable master? It's about double what the horse is worth, but I want him to have the cash. I know it would ease her mind."

A gentle smile lifted her lips. "I would be honored."

"I should go. It's very nice to meet you." He paused at the door, not sure what moved him to speak again. "Your daughter is an amazing woman."

A knowing grin lifted the edges of her lips. "Thank you, Mr. Lancaster. I could not agree more."

He walked out the door. On instinct, his eyes searched the surrounding countryside traveling over the valleys and hills to ensure he remained undetected. With his mind settled and his heart at peace, Luke leaped into the saddle and headed toward town.

He only had a couple of days to make arrangements before the showdown.

~*~

Luke relaxed in a chair at his favorite restaurant, enjoying a warm, buttered corn tortilla along with a scrambled egg topped with onion, jalapeno, and tomatoes. He'd barely finished eating when the newspaper publisher sauntered in.

Laurence plopped down in the chair opposite Luke and gave Luke a pointed glare. "This better be good. It's a dusty trail from El Paso to Justice City, and my clothes have not fared well."

"How predictable," Luke said, almost smiling. "Here I am offering you a major news story, and you're annoyed because of a little dust on your garments. Perhaps I should have left you alone—let you find out after the fact."

"I'm not sure I trust you. Remember our last meeting?"

"As I recall, you did me a favor."

Laurence glanced over his shoulder. "It's only a matter of time before Sheriff McGregor and his deputies come looking for you. I'd rather not be in close proximity when that happens."

"And that's why I need your help."

Laurence dipped his chin. "Why should I help you?"

"Because it gives you a chance to do the right thing and have a first-hand account of the story."

"I'm intrigued. I admit. As a newspaperman and an investigator, I'd like to hear what you propose. But I will not risk my life for you, Luke. That I can promise."

"I'm not asking you to, but I do need your word that you won't tell a soul."

Laurence leaned in closer—an eager grin upon his lips. "You have my word."

~*~

Billie walked up and down the winding, hilly streets of the quaint Arkansas town, stepping into the clothing store to purchase a ready-made dress or two and a couple of bonnets. She couldn't keep wearing the same clothes every day. She selected one dress in a pale daffodil color for church and another in a dove gray, which was more suitable for teaching attire. Both only needed minor alterations to fit.

Her uncle had offered her money to help her make the purchases, and she'd accepted. Although she had money saved, she could not get to it yet. Soon, she hoped, she could contact her mother and have all her funds transferred to the local bank. Then she could pay her uncle back every cent, whether he would accept or not.

She'd barely made it past a few of the shops when someone approached from behind. She turned, looking back over her shoulder to see a man giving her an attentive gaze. Her heart raced. He wore a gun and had the hard look of someone out to do no good. Billie walked a little faster, but he kept pace. Finally, when she thought she'd take off running, the man whistled and waved to someone across the street.

"Hey, Joe! Wait up."

Her legs froze, stiffness traveling up her entire body.

The man's spurs jingled as he scurried across the street, greeting his friend with a slap on the back and then guiding him into the general store.

"For goodness sake..." Billie muttered under her breath, feeling outright silly. Her hand rested on her chest, calming her runaway heart. *I can't live like this, Lord—always wondering, always afraid. Please, Father, move on my behalf. Help Luke help me, but most of all, keep him safe.*

Her uncle loomed ahead of her loading grain into the buggy with a heavy grunt. Billie hurried toward him, thankful for a friendly face and eager to return to the ranch.

"This here is Amos," her uncle said, pointing to a large young man with a bag of grain hoisted across his shoulder.

Amos laid the bag in the buckboard as if it were a feather. The man didn't even break a sweat. The sack would be impossible for her to carry and almost impossible for her uncle.

"Amos lived at the ranch until about six months ago." Uncle Rupert extended his palm her direction. "This is my niece, Miss Billie Jo Batson."

"Your uncle done told me all about you." Amos smiled from ear to ear. "The Schumann Ranch is one of a kind in these parts. Taught me respect for myself, respect for my peers, and respect for the Word of God. It's a good thing you're doing with them boys, Miss Billie. A mighty good thing. No one has to tell you, but God is pleased."

His words washed over her like a warm wave of

crystal-clear water. Wasn't that all she ever wanted to do? Make a difference in a young person's life. That was what drew her to teaching.

"You're pretty young still, Amos. Why aren't you living at the ranch?"

"I was adopted by the Barker family. They had a son, but he ran off, got married, and then took off with a traveling theater group. The Barkers needed help with the chores and told me if I'd be their son, they'd adopt me and take real good care of me. So far, that's what they've done."

"But your education—"

"I still go to school part of the time. I already know my numbers and my letters." He grinned. "But if you want me to come out to the ranch and learn more, I can ask. I just don't want to give up my family to do it."

"I'm glad to hear you're happy." She smiled. "That's important. And as long as you're continuing your education, even if only part-time, I'm sure you'll do fine in life."

"Yes, ma'am. That's what Mrs. Matilda said, too. 'Keep bettering yourself, Amos, and one day you'll look back and be real proud.'" He grinned. "I'm already real proud."

"I'm glad I got to meet you today. You've given me something to think about."

"Something good, I hope," he said, adding a chuckle.

Maybe staying at the ranch and running the place was not such a bad idea after all. Amos' words showed that better lives improved self-esteem, and a sense of purpose was as important as learning letters and numbers.

"Would you like to join us for supper tonight?" Billie asked, hoping her uncle wouldn't object.

"I think I would. It's been too long since I talked to Mrs. Matilda and ate some of her black-eyed peas."

"How'd you know we'd be having black-eyed peas?" Uncle Rupert asked, giving Amos a poke with his elbow that caused the younger man to chuckle.

"Mrs. Matilda has black-eyed peas for every supper."

"We'll save you a place at the table." Billie grinned.

Uncle Rupert helped her into the buggy before taking the reins and giving them a gentle flick. "You certainly took charge back there. I think you'll work out fine in your new job."

Billie shook her head in amusement but did not object. The notion was starting to sound good to her.

24

Luke waited for Laurence to approach.

"I did what you said," Laurence began, looking up and down the streets. Perspiration dotted his forehead and his wide-eyed gaze locked upon Luke.

"And?" Luke asked.

"Clovis Caldwell swallowed it like a crow eating a one-legged beetle." He lifted his chin and grinned, a look of self-satisfaction upon his features. "This is rather exciting. I see now how a person could get drawn to your lifestyle."

"This isn't a game. Lives are at stake."

"It is a game, in a way."

Luke's stare turned stern. He could see that Laurence had no idea he was playing with fire. "What'd Clovis say?"

"After I explained to him that I was a news reporter from El Paso wanting to do a story on the female fugitive who'd run off with his money and a well-known bounty hunter, he was all ears. Then when I told him where my sources said they were hiding; he ended the interview."

"Good. And is he headed there now?"

"Yes. He rode out of town. Along with the sheriff,

his deputy, and a half a dozen or more men."

"Perfect." Luke patted Laurence on the back. "You'll get the exclusive story. I've got to hurry—"

"Don't you mean *we* have to hurry."

"Laurence, I don't want your blood on my hands."

"You don't think I can take care of myself?"

"No. Frankly, I don't."

"Well, you're wrong." He pulled a small derringer from his coat pocket. "I am armed."

Luke grinned. "Shoot someone with that little thing, and it'll only make them mad."

"I don't want to kill anyone. I only want to stop them from doing away with me."

"All right. You can come but stay out of the way. These men are dangerous. Don't let them see you, or they'll kill you."

"You've made your point. Now let's get on with it."

Luke followed a good distance behind Clovis Caldwell, Sheriff McGregor, the undercover deputy, and the other men. He'd lured them to the Valley of Bones—a place he knew well and trusted would give him the upper hand.

After traveling for an hour with the sun blazing across the West Texas sky and the hot wind in their face, the men finally stopped. They stood in the middle of a small valley where bones lay about—it was the place where the Indians burned their dead horses.

Luke sat in the saddle at the crest of the ridge, examining the terrain. After a silent prayer, he flicked his reins and moved down the rocky path into the sunken valley. He'd instructed Laurence to remain out of sight, no matter the outcome. Even though they argued and bantered back and forth, he did not want anything to happen to the man.

Luke drew his horse to a complete stop in front of a stranger. "Are you Clovis Caldwell?"

"So, we finally meet."

Clovis was a tall man—much taller and older in appearance than the sheriff. He sat rather regal in the saddle with muscled legs wrapped around his horse's belly. Fine clothes covered his form in tailored perfection. Silver hair lay in thick waves against his scalp. From all appearances, he was a man of means. Only the brittle coldness in his eyes hinted at the depravity of his soul.

Luke's gaze shifted toward the sheriff. "McGregor."

Sheriff McGregor twirled a grain stem about his mouth, maneuvering it from one side of his lips to the other. "Howdy. Again."

Luke glanced at the undercover deputy, hoping for some sign of recognition but receiving nothing that brought him comfort. The kid was too young to be on an assignment. Barely old enough to be out of school. Why had Theo sent a boy to do such an important job?

"And you are?" Luke asked, determined to play his part well.

"Don't matter about him," Sheriff McGregor spat. "You're gonna die today, mister. There ain't any need to go makin' new friends."

Clovis exhaled. "Never was one for being subtle,

were you McGregor?"

"Why am I going to die?" Luke asked. His calmness rattled the men around him. They expected fear. That's what they were used to getting when they intimidated people. He wasn't afraid, but neither was he foolish. He intended to control the outcome to the best of his ability. There was more at stake than his life. He had Billie Jo to think about. "Is it because I know the truth—that you were the one stealing the gold from your own bank—not Billie Jo or Malcolm?"

Clovis snickered.

"You think you're smart, don't you?" McGregor taunted.

"Billie Jo's trying to keep a noose off her neck," Clovis said. "She'd say anything to spare her life. She and I both know she's guilty."

"I don't think so."

"Dead men don't get an opinion," Clovis replied.

The undercover deputy pulled his gun. "Want me to end this right now?"

What is he doing? Trying to get me killed?

"Not yet." Clovis took control with ease. "I already told you. I need to know where she's hiding." His gaze pierced Luke's own. "So unless you'd like to die really slow—"

"Why do you care?" Luke asked. "If you're innocent, let her go. Her crimes will catch up with her. Of course, if you're trying to hide something, I can see why you might want to find her and make sure she never talks."

"I've not got anything to hide." Clovis didn't even

flinch.

Luke glared. "You took that gold, didn't you? It was a brilliant plan. Get innocent people to work for you and then steal the miners' gold but blame the only other person who had access to the vault." He chuckled. "I'll hand it to you. Not everyone could've come up with something that smart."

Clovis's chin dipped downward. A smugness lifted the edges of his lips, so faint that Luke would not have noticed if he'd not been looking at every expression and movement. Luke shrugged. "If I'm going to die anyway, then why not tell the truth?"

"I'm not telling you anything. Why should I?"

Luke glanced from Clovis to Sheriff McGregor. "Or were you the mastermind behind the theft? I didn't peg you for the smart one, but maybe I'm wrong. Maybe you're the one who came up with the idea in the first place."

Clovis chuckled, the sound grating against the tension in the air. "You don't think McGregor could pull this off, do you?"

Sheriff McGregor's chest puffed outward. "Wait a minute—"

Just as Luke figured. Clovis Caldwell's ego wouldn't let him ignore the bait. There was no way he would let McGregor or anyone else take credit for his conniving.

"I did take the gold," Clovis continued, his eyes opened wide in a mad stare. "I'll take even more if I want, and if anyone gets in my way—"

"What's got into you?" Sheriff McGregor asked in

a scolding tone. "Now ain't the time to go confessing."

"The man's as good as dead," Clovis declared. "We'll leave his body here. Everyone will think the Comanches got him."

"I'm not the least bit concerned about him," McGregor exclaimed, his face now splotchy with anger. When Clovis only stared, the sheriff continued in a rage. "You think you're the smart one? Well, I think it takes a real idiot to confess in front of a group of people—unless you plan on killing every single person here."

Clovis lifted his gun out of his holster and shot the sheriff in the chest, killing him instantly. McGregor rolled out of his saddle onto the ground.

The deputy's face paled.

Luke stared in stunned silence.

The posse behind them tugged on their horse's reins—backing up several paces. A couple of the men put their hands on their gun handles.

As much as Luke tried to prepare himself, there was no way to prepare for the unpredictable madness of a man consumed by greed. He prayed Laurence would not scream or take off running for the hills. If he did, he'd be as good as dead. Hopefully, he was as shocked as the rest of them and remained petrified in disbelief.

"Like I was saying before I was interrupted—" Clovis straightened his coat jacket with his free arm, leveling his gun on Luke. "I ordered the sheriff to shoot Malcolm dead. But that doesn't concern you. You're not getting out of here alive."

"I beg to differ. You're the one not getting out alive."

"You're going to stop me?" Clovis chuckled. "Did you not witness what just happened to McGregor?"

"I won't do anything to you." Luke looked up onto the ridge of the hillside. "But they might. You're on animal burial grounds, and my Comanche brothers don't take kindly to your disrespect. They're watching you right now. All I have to do is give the signal."

"What signal?"

"Are you sure you want me to show you?" Luke taunted, looking upward into the hillside once more. "If I do—"

"You think I'm stupid enough to turn around?"

"No. I think you're stupid enough to sit right where you're at and get an arrow in the back. Just like you deserve."

Clovis turned around to look at an empty hillside. When he did, Luke leaped forward in the saddle—knocking him off his horse and sending them both crashing to the hard ground. Luke straddled Clovis, pinning his arms to the ground—squeezing his wrist until he screamed and released the gun.

"What are you waiting on?" Clovis wailed in fury at the men with him. "Kill him!" Not a single man moved. "Cowards! Every one of you! Shoot him!"

"Not after you shot the sheriff," one man said. "No telling which one of us would be next. Come on, boys. Let's get out of here."

Clovis let out a loud curse into the air.

Luke lifted him to his feet, wrestling his hands

behind him.

The undercover deputy stepped forward with rope and tied Caldwell's wrists behind his back in a hard knot. "That was a close one," the deputy said.

"I thought you were going to kill me back there."

"Just playing my part."

The man was better than Luke had given him credit. Maybe Theo did know what he was doing.

Shock darkened Clovis's features as he stared at the young deputy. "You're with *him*?"

"Yep," Luke said with a firm bob of his head. "Let's head back to the jail." He turned toward the undercover deputy. "Can you carry McGregor's body on your horse? I don't want to leave it here for the buzzards."

Laurence appeared from behind a tree, his voice quivering. "I'm all right. Yes, I'm all right." He pointed toward Clovis with a trembling finger. "And you, sir, deserve a noose around your neck."

Clovis remained silent, a sense of defeat surrounding his formerly pompous demeanor.

"Finally—" Luke fixed his gaze upon Laurence Magellan. "Something we can agree upon."

25

Billie stood outside in the fresh air and sunshine, discussing the possibility of expanding the garden. It was not easy running a house with so many boys, and she'd already talked to Uncle Rupert about hiring someone later on to help with the cooking and cleaning. For now, she enjoyed working herself into exhaustion. It was the only way to keep her mind from coming undone with thoughts and hopes that would never come to pass.

A golden glow dusted the hillside in quiet beauty, and though she wanted to stay in the mid-afternoon breeze and relax, there was more work waiting. Her eyes lingered upon the road that led to their ranch. She'd settled into her routine during the last few months, but her heart still longed for what might have been with Luke.

The practical side of her soul said to leave it alone. The emotional side demanded she pull it out and examine every second of every memory for some hint of what their life could have been like if he'd stayed. At times, she let her emotions have their say, but for the most part, she kept busy.

The boys adjusted and even thrived in the routine,

in part because they all knew ahead of time what they'd do every day. Aunt Matilda spent her hours telling funny stories from her childhood, shelling pecans, snapping peas, canning peaches, and teaching the young men to read from the Bible. It gave her tremendous joy, which blessed Billie's heart as well.

Billie arched her back, stretching out the tightness that knotted the muscles along her spine. She'd about scrubbed the hide off her fingers from cleaning sheets earlier in the day. The boys didn't seem to mind rolling around in the dust then carrying the dirt and grime into bed, but she intended to change that habit.

"From now on," Billie began, talking to her uncle. "I want the boys to all wash in the stream before getting into bed. I've never seen such filth, and I have several brothers, so don't tell me this is normal. If it's too cold for them, they can take a bath indoors."

Uncle Rupert laughed, shrugging his shoulders as if he'd got caught with his hand in the cookie jar. "I don't know about that, Billie Jo. Sunday is wash day. If I tell them every day is wash day, we might have a mutiny."

"At least they can wash their hands, faces, and feet before crawling into bed. I don't think that's too much to ask."

"I admit, these boys lack proper hygiene. Maybe we need to add a class on that subject to the schedule?"

"You know, that's a great idea," Billie exclaimed. "I'm surprised I didn't think of it."

Uncle Rupert shook his head, laughter spilling from his lips.

"We can teach them about—" She stopped in midsentence, staring down the road. She couldn't make out the rider, but a familiar horse moved toward the entry gate. Her heart slammed into her chest. "Uncle Rupert. Is that—"

"I believe so." A wide grin busted across his lips. "I told you he'd be back."

Billie remained planted right where she stood. Uncle Rupert made some excuse then disappeared inside the cabin. Her stomach twisted and turned in excitement while her knees melted like taffy in the hot August sun.

She reached out, braced against a tree, and spoke out loud into the heavens. "Dear Lord, let this be what I long for or make my heart grow numb. I can't do this again..."

~*~

Luke rode his horse down the path in slow motion—swaying in the saddle and determined not to rush the moment. He'd done such a good job of convincing himself that he and Billie should not be together, he feared she'd done the same.

As he neared the cabin, he noticed her outside. Sheets hung nearby on a makeshift clothesline—the cloth flapping in the breeze. Several chickens roamed about the yard, pecking at the ground.

Luke's heart thrashed about. He'd looked down the barrel of many a gun without flinching. He'd stood toe-to-toe with some of the vilest outlaws alive. And yet, the thought of the conversation he was about to have with Billie Jo unnerved him. His insides turned to water.

Even from a distance, her hair shimmered in the sunlight and a hopeful expression rested upon porcelain features. Her countenance should give him courage, but the opposite happened. His insides shriveled up into a marble at the mere sight of her.

Had he been gone too long? Did she belong to another? Was she only eager to see him because she longed to hear news about her accusers, and whether her name was cleared?

Luke drew his horse to a halt near her. He slid out of the saddle then stopped, wondering what he would say. Before he could think another thought, Billie rushed toward him, a smile upon her lips and tears of joy spilling down her cheeks.

His arms drew her up against him—inhaling the fragrance of her hair and succumbing to the softness of her flesh. She pressed into him, her cheek against his chest and her arms locked behind his back.

"You're alive!"

He nuzzled her ear with his lips, whispering her name. "Billie Jo…"

Her hands moved around to rest upon his chest as dewy eyes, the color of the bluest skies, searched his face.

Any remaining resolve collapsed. "Billie Jo, I love you."

"I love you, too."

"I don't want to leave you. Not ever again. Will

you be my wife?"

Her entire body rose and fell against him. "Yes…"

He lowered his lips to her own, tasting the sweetness of love—the kind of love given with abandon. The kind of love that let him know that his life would never be the same, and he'd be a better man because of it. At that moment, nothing else mattered. Not the past pain. Not the job he left. Nothing. Because nothing compared to what he felt for Billie Jo. His kiss deepened, and he heard a sweet groan sift from between her lips. He could hardly wait to make her his—all of her.

Cheering erupted from behind him.

Luke drew the kiss to a tender close. He looked over his shoulder, seeing all twenty or so boys standing outside their cabin—clapping, whistling, and laughing.

"Looks like we get to plan a wedding, boys," Freddy called out.

~*~

"My name is cleared?"

"Yes. Clovis Caldwell is in jail, awaiting trial. Sheriff McGregor is dead—murdered by Clovis in front of a handful of witnesses."

"Justice is served," Uncle Rupert said, taking a sip of coffee. Aunt Matilda refilled his cup, adding a bit more to her own before returning to her seat.

"I can finally write to my parents and not worry about their safety."

"I made a special trip to Justice City so I could let your parents know you were safe," Luke said.

Billie lay her hand upon his. She was grateful for such a thoughtful act.

"Now you'll have to write them about the wedding," Aunt Matilda said. "I'm sure your parents will want to be here. And your brothers, too."

"Along with Abigail, Henry, my father. And my aunt Louise."

"Whatever compelled that man to think he'd get away with it?" Uncle Rupert scratched his head. "He already had so much."

"Isn't that how greed works? It demands more and more."

Uncle Rupert nodded his head. "That is true, young man, and now, I'd like to go over something with you—something I think you'll like."

Billie's insides tighten. She wasn't sure how Luke would react to Uncle Rupert's plans. Would he be thankful and see it as a gift from God, or would he feel offended—as if no one thought he could take care of his future wife. She moved to the edge of her seat, fingers grasping the cushion.

Uncle Rupert's brow twisted downward in thought. "Matilda and I aren't exactly spring chickens. We want to do less and less around here. But we need a young married couple who'd be willing to take over the ranch and raise about twenty or so boys. Do you think that's a chore you'd like to take on?"

Luke sat up straighter. "I don't know. It doesn't seem fair that you worked for this your whole life, and then to put someone else in charge—"

"I'm not putting someone else in charge. I'm giving you the place. God gifted me with this property for the boys' ranch. As a good steward, part of my job is to find the next person to take over—someone who loves the ranch and the boys and will take good care of them." He beamed. "I think God brought the right couple to me."

Luke stood up. His expression was filled with amazement. "I don't know what to say."

"Yes would be a good start," Uncle Rupert teased.

"A thousand times, yes," Luke exclaimed.

"Very well. We'll meet with the attorney and make all the arrangements after the wedding." Uncle Rupert rose, turning a loving smile to his wife. "Let's leave these lovebirds alone, my dear. They've got much to discuss, and we'll only be in the way."

Aunt Matilda rose, bending over to kiss Billie on the top of the head, and then looking her in the eye. "God can turn all things to good, can't He?"

The heat of tears lingered in her gaze as she bobbed her head. "All things."

Epilogue

Luke inhaled the scent of spring. Wildflowers and dogwood trees dotted the Arkansas countryside. A copper-haired toddler ran through the tall, feather-like grass, chasing butterflies and laughing at nothing in particular.

He approached Billie Jo with a hammer in his hand and soreness across his shoulders. She stood under the shade of a tree, her eyes upon their daughter.

"I'm done driving fence posts for the day. Freddy and the boys are headed back in to clean up for supper."

"According to Lilith, we're having butterfly soup for supper." Billie looked at their young daughter.

He grinned. "My favorite."

"Mine, too, Daddy," Lilith exclaimed as she ran by, leaping and jumping for butterflies but always coming up empty-handed.

In the quiet shade with only a faint breeze, something stirred inside his being that he'd never felt before: *contentment*. He saw the same reflected upon his wife's unguarded expression.

The ghosts of his past and the ghost of Billie's past

had laid down together, buried and put to rest. Neither would forget the loved ones they lost, but they no longer shouldered the guilt. The Lord had lifted their burden and poured forth his healing balm—the peace that passes all understanding.

"The boys want to know if they can help your parents with their barn raising." He propped his foot upon a stump. "They know there'll be lots of people there—including pretty girls from church."

She was thankful she'd convinced her parents to join them on the ranch. She was still trying to convince her brothers to join in the work, knowing that would bring joy to her mother and father. Perhaps one day …

"Do you think that's wise?" Billie asked. "If they start thinking about girls, they won't think about their studies, or working, or— I'm afraid I'm too hard on them, aren't I?"

"You expect a lot, but I think we both know they're fine young men. It'll be OK if they have a little fun."

"All right, then. But I insist they wear their Sunday clothes."

Silence lay between them for several seconds, both lost in the rustling of the tree branches and the beauty of a child's laughter.

"Think we'll always be this happy, Luke?"

He lay his hand around her waist. She was already expecting again, and he couldn't be happier. "We'll have our ups and downs, but I love you, and we're right where we're supposed to be—taking care of these boys and running this ranch."

They both worked hard, but it was work he'd always wanted to do. His wife flourished as she taught, and the boys learned more than he ever thought possible under her guidance.

Abigail, Henry, Henry, Jr., and the twins—Sarah and May—had visited twice. Walking Stick always journeyed with them. Aunt Louise had only made it down for the wedding, passing away the following year from pneumonia.

He'd not spoken to Theo after picking up his final pay along with a nice bonus from the insurance company. He'd heard his former boss got the promotion he wanted and currently resided in Pennsylvania.

Laurence Magellan wrote him one letter, letting him know that he missed writing stories about him but thanked him for his treatment of prisoners over the years. He even wrote an entire article about his departure from bounty hunting in the *El Paso Tribune*, recognizing his exploits with more blarney than a leprechaun's tall tales.

One of the greatest gifts he'd received since his life changed was a box from Mighty Bow. It just appeared on his doorstep one day. The war chief had given him an ornamental knife that once belonged to his grandfather. He knew it was the old chief's way of making amends.

Though Luke admitted that his life had twisted and turned, sometimes in the wrong direction, the final destination had brought him right where he wanted to be and right where God always intended—with Billie and the fatherless boys he would help parent. His eyes looked toward the heavens and he smiled. "Thank You, Lord."

Only feet away, his daughter laughed.

Entwined in the laughter, Luke heard the faintest whisper in his heart.

"You're welcome."

A Devotional Moment

Those who with a word make someone out to be guilty, who ensnare the defender in court and with false testimony deprive the innocent of justice. ~ Isaiah 29:21

It is not hard to understand why lying is so insidious when people do it all the time. "Little white lies" are considered expedient in our society. People lie about how clothing looks on someone, about where they were at a specific time, about what they were doing in the past. But when we lie habitually, as most of us know, one small lie leads to bigger ones. "False witness" is a lie in which another's life can be destroyed with one wrong word. We've all heard stories of people whose lives were ruined by another's lie. People go to jail for crimes they didn't commit, because someone lied. People get out of jail and are unable to get jobs or help, because despite proving innocence, there are those who always have a little niggle of doubt. Justice isn't served.

In **The Bounty Hunter's Bride**, the protagonist is accused of a crime she didn't commit. She escapes to stay free because it's the only way she can prove her innocence. But the real criminals and the law are both out to get her. When she has to place her trust in another, God shows a plan that will redeem both her and her own protagonist.

Have you ever been the victim of false witness? If so, you know how harmful it can be, but even more harmful is the tendency to bear a grudge and become hard-hearted and cynical. This is one reason why God tells you to pray for your enemies and to forgive. . .not for them, but for your sake.

If you've ever lied about someone else, or allowed a lie to live on so you could protect yourself, it's time to repent. The damage done by those lies might never be fully rectified, but you can repent and do your best to undo the harm done.

LORD, HELP ME NEVER TO PERPETRATE OR ALLOW LIES AND DECEIT TO BE SPOKEN AGAINST OTHERS. HELP ME ALSO TO FORGIVE THOSE WHO HAVE WRONGED ME. IN JESUS' NAME I PRAY, AMEN.

Thank you

We appreciate you reading this White Rose Publishing title. For other inspirational stories, please visit our on-line bookstore at www.pelicanbookgroup.com.

For questions or more information, contact us at customer@pelicanbookgroup.com.

White Rose Publishing
Where Faith is the Cornerstone of Love™
an imprint of Pelican Book Group
www.PelicanBookGroup.com

Connect with Us
www.facebook.com/Pelicanbookgroup
www.twitter.com/pelicanbookgrp

To receive news and specials, subscribe to our bulletin
http://pelink.us/bulletin

May God's glory shine through
this inspirational work of fiction.

AMDG

You Can Help!

At Pelican Book Group it is our mission to entertain readers with fiction that uplifts the Gospel. It is our privilege to spend time with you awhile as you read our stories.

We believe you can help us to bring Christ into the lives of people across the globe. And you don't have to open your wallet or even leave your house!

Here are 3 simple things you can do to help us bring illuminating fiction™ to people everywhere.

1) If you enjoyed this book, write a positive review. Post it at online retailers and websites where readers gather. And share your review with us at reviews@pelicanbookgroup.com (this does give us permission to reprint your review in whole or in part.)

2) If you enjoyed this book, recommend it to a friend in person, at a book club or on social media.

3) If you have suggestions on how we can improve or expand our selection, let us know. We value your opinion. Use the contact form on our web site or e-mail us at customer@pelicanbookgroup.com

God Can Help!

Are you in need? The Almighty can do great things for you. Holy is His Name! He has mercy in every generation. He can lift up the lowly and accomplish all things. Reach out today.

Do not fear: I am with you; do not be anxious: I am your God. I will strengthen you, I will help you, I will uphold you with my victorious right hand.

~Isaiah 41:10 (NAB)

We pray daily, and we especially pray for everyone connected to Pelican Book Group—that includes you! If you have a specific need, we welcome the opportunity to pray for you. Share your needs or praise reports at http://pelink.us/pray4us

Free eBook Offer

We're looking for booklovers like you to partner with us! Join our team of influencers today and periodically receive free eBooks!

For more information
Visit http://pelicanbookgroup.com/booklovers

How About Free Audiobooks?

We're looking for audiobook lovers, too! Partner with us as an audiobook lover and periodically receive free audiobooks!

For more information
Visit
http://pelicanbookgroup.com/booklovers/freeaudio.html

or e-mail
booklovers@pelicanbookgroup.com